"Marry me,"

Luke whispered urgently against her neck.

For a moment Sherri wondered if she'd only imagined the words.

He took her by the shoulders. "Let's get married again, Sherri."

"You're crazy," she whispered incredulously, so afraid to hope.

"What's so crazy about it? We're good together. Let's give Danny what he really wants. The two of us together again. Let's do it for him."

"Just because we're good together in bed isn't a reason to rush to the nearest justice of the peace." Her voice shook, and tears burned sharply in her eyes. "I think we let our emotions over Danny get all twisted and out of control. To take this any further would be an even bigger mistake."

He smiled. "But it's still good between us."

"It will probably always be good between us... but that doesn't make it right."

Dear Reader,

Where's the best place to find love this holiday season? UNDER THE MISTLETOE! This month, Silhouette Romance brings you a special collection of stories filled with spirited romance and holiday cheer.

'Tis the season for Christmas wishes, and nine-year-old Danny Morgan has a tall order. He wants to reunite his divorced parents. Will FABULOUS FATHER Luke Morgan be able to win ex-wife Sherri Morgan's love—and fulfill his son's dreams? Find out in Carla Cassidy's heartwarming romance, *Anything for Danny*.

Helen R. Myers brings us a wonderful romance about the power of true love. *To Wed at Christmas* is David Shepherd and Harmony Martin's wish—though their feuding families struggle to keep them apart.

Linda Varner continues the trilogy, MR. RIGHT, INC. with *Believing in Miracles*. Falling in love again may be out of the question for single dad Andy Fulbright. But when he meets Honey Truman, *marriage* isn't....

Look for more love and cheer with a charming book from Toni Collins. *Miss Scrooge* may not have much Christmas spirit, but it's nothing that a holiday with sexy Gabe Wheeler can't cure. Lucinda Lambert is running from danger when she finds protection and love in the arms of *A Cowboy for Christmas*. Look for this emotional romance by Stella Bagwell. And Lynn Bulock rounds out the month with the delightful *Surprise Package*.

Wishing you a happy holiday and wonderful New Year!

Anne Canadeo
Senior Editor

Please address questions and book requests to:
Silhouette Reader Service
U.S.: 3010 Walden Ave., P.O. Box 1325, Buffalo, NY 14269
Canadian: P.O. Box 609, Fort Erie, Ont. L2A 5X3

ANYTHING FOR DANNY

Carla Cassidy

Silhouette
R O M A N C E™
Published by Silhouette Books
America's Publisher of Contemporary Romance

To my Dad. Your courage inspired, your laughter
enlivened, your love warmed me through the years.
I love you, big man!

 SILHOUETTE BOOKS

ISBN 0-373-19048-4

ANYTHING FOR DANNY

Copyright © 1994 by Carla Bracale

Books by Carla Cassidy

Silhouette Romance

Patchwork Family #818
Whatever Alex Wants... #856
Fire and Spice #884
Homespun Hearts #905
Golden Girl #924
Something New #942
Pixie Dust #958
The Littlest Matchmaker #978
The Marriage Scheme #996
Anything for Danny #1048

Silhouette Desire

A Fleeting Moment #784
Under the Boardwalk #882

Silhouette Shadows

Swamp Secrets #4
Heart of the Beast #11
Silent Screams #25

Silhouette Intimate Moments

One of the Good Guys #531
Try To Remember #560
Fugitive Father #604

Silhouette Books

Silhouette Shadows
short stories 1993

"Devil and the Deep Blue Sea"

The Loop

Getting It Right: Jessica

CARLA CASSIDY

is the author of ten young-adult novels, as well as many contemporary romances. She's been a cheerleader for the Kansas City Chiefs football team and has traveled the East Coast as a singer and dancer in a band, but the greatest pleasure she's had is in creating romance and happiness for readers.

Dear Santa Claus,

Before I tell you what I want this year for Christmas, I want to thank you for bringing me that super model of a Boeing B-17 Flying Fortress bomber plane last year. It took me a long time to put it together and now it's hanging over my bed.

This year I've got something harder in mind, but it's something I want really, really bad. I'd like it if you could please do whatever you can to get my mom and dad back together again. I know, it's going to be a tough job, but they belong with each other. We need to be a family again and I know *you* can pull it off if anyone can.

I'm just a kid, but I know Mom and Dad still love each other. Grown-ups can be pretty dumb, huh? I would *really* be happy if you could do this for me as soon as possible.

Yours truly,

Danny Morgan

Danny L. Morgan

Chapter One

"Sherri, you can't be serious about this," Margaret, Sherri Morgan's best friend, said in dismay.

"I'm very serious about it." Sherri poured Margaret another glass of iced tea, then rejoined her at the kitchen table. "You know what this means to Danny."

"Yes, but a cross-country trip in a motor home...in the winter...with Luke...it's madness, sheer madness." Margaret frowned and twirled a strand of her shoulder-length blond hair. "Mark my words, it's madness."

Sherri smiled ruefully. "It probably is, but Luke and I have agreed that if this is what Danny wants, then we'll give it to him. Besides, with three weeks of Christmas vacation from school, it's the best time to go."

"But I thought you and Luke barely speak to each other, that there was all kinds of bad blood between you."

"We speak," Sherri replied. "We don't see each other often but when we do we're always civil and polite. As far as bad blood...it's been five years since our divorce. I don't hold any grudges. I have my life and he has his."

"I still say the whole idea is crazy. What are you going to do if you get snowed in someplace?"

"Dig out," Sherri returned with a grin.

Margaret frowned. "What did the doctor say? Is Danny really well enough to make the trip?"

Sherri's smile trembled slightly. "Dr. Winthrope says if we're going to do it, now is the time. Danny's stabilized for the moment, but who knows how long it will last?" A sharp stab of pain pierced her heart as she thought of her nine-year-old son.

Sweet Danny with the sunshine smile and overwhelming enthusiasm for life. Cheerful Danny...her life. His diagnosis of leukemia a year before had thrown her world topsy-turvy. "Anyway," she continued, shoving these sad thoughts aside, "it's all set. With both Danny and me on Christmas vacation and the weather so unusually mild, there's no reason not to go. We leave first thing in the morning."

"Well, I think the whole thing is crazy," Margaret repeated once again. "Can you put up with Luke for three weeks in the cramped confines of a motor home?" Margaret eyed her skeptically.

Sherri slowly nodded. "Sure. I can put up with anything for any amount of time for Danny," she replied with grim determination. "Even Luke."

"Hey, Mom, it's here!" Danny's excited voice drifted in through the kitchen window. "Come out and see. It's here. It's here!"

"Goodness, what's he talking about?" Margaret looked at Sherri curiously. "You'd think the Goodyear blimp just parked on your front yard."

Sherri laughed. "Not the Goodyear blimp... the motor home. The people from the Dream Producers said it would be delivered some time this morning. Come on, we'd better get out there or Danny will have a fit."

Together the two women grabbed their coats, left the kitchen and walked out into the early-morning Connecticut sunshine. Sherri stepped off the porch, then stopped and caught her breath as she eyed the shining vehicle parked along the curb in front of the house.

It was bright blue, with the Dream Producer's logo on the side. It was huge. It was a monstrosity. It looked more like a house than a vehicle. And that's exactly what it would be for the next three weeks, their home on wheels.

"Hi, Sherri." The driver, one of the volunteers from the Dream Producers Charity, got out of the motor home and gave her a jaunty salute.

"Hi, Ross," she greeted him warmly. Over the past several weeks Sherri had grown close to all the volunteers who'd worked so diligently to make Danny's dream wish come true.

"Here are the keys, an instruction manual and an itinerary and map that will take you to the Grand Canyon." He handed her the items. "We've marked the campsites that are close to area hospitals and also tourist attractions that are open year-round that we thought might interest Danny. We've also got a weather radio inside the R.V. so you can find out about weather conditions." He frowned, eyeing Sherri's slender arms and short stature. "You sure you can handle driving this baby?"

Sherri nodded confidently. "My family took a trip with a motor home the summer I was sixteen. I did a lot of the driving." She smiled at Ross. "I don't know how to thank you...how to thank all of you." She took Ross's hand in hers and held it close. "You've all done so much for us...for Danny."

"The best thanks is to give that boy the trip of his dreams." Ross patted her hand and released it. "Make yourself and that boy some precious memories. That's all the thanks we need."

"Hey, Mom, come on in...this is awesome!" Danny's voice rang from one of the windows of the huge R.V. "There's a bathroom and bedroom and everything. Margaret, come on in and see everything. Mom, come on!"

Ross laughed. "Go on, he's waiting to show you around." He paused and smiled at Sherri once again, a bittersweet smile. "That Danny, he's a special kind of kid."

She nodded, a lump forming in her throat as she remembered that Ross had lost his thirteen-year-old son the year before to bone marrow cancer.

"Go on, go to him. Make every moment count. Make some memories." Ross's eyes were over-bright as he gave her arm a quick squeeze, then went to the car that waited to take him back to the Dream Producers headquarters.

Sherri hesitated a moment, swallowing the emotions that lately were always too close to the surface, the tears that always pressed against her eyes.

It was a rule... Danny's rule. No crying allowed. From the moment they had learned the extent of his illness, he'd been firm in his demand of no crying where he could see it or hear it. In the months that had passed, she had grown quite proficient at silent weeping, usually at night into her pillow.

"Mom!" Danny's voice cried out impatiently.

"All right, all right, I'm coming," Sherri exclaimed. She stepped into the motor home, and looked around in amazement. It *was* like a miniature home. There was a table with a bench seat, a stove, a small refrigerator and wooden cabinets just behind the four captain's chairs.

"Mom, come here," Danny called from the back of the vehicle.

Sherri passed the bathroom complete with stall shower, then entered the back area, where Danny sat on the top bunk, and Margaret was on the bottom bunk. "This is so cool." Danny's eyes were bright with excitement, their blueness perfectly matching the ball cap on top of his head. "Look, there are little cubby-holes up here to put stuff."

"The whole interior has been customized," Margaret commented.

Sherri nodded, noting the unusually wide entrance to the bathroom. "They've customized it so it can accommodate wheelchairs," she observed. "The space around the table is also larger than usual."

"Can I sleep up here? Can this be my bed?" Danny asked.

"I don't know, we'll have to wait and see." Lord, she hadn't even thought of the sleeping arrangements. There were two beds, the top bunk and the bottom, and although both were nearly double size, there was no way Danny would have one of those bunks to himself, leaving her and Luke to share the other.

"Madness," Margaret repeated, as if reading Sherri's thoughts. "I told you this was all crazy."

Sherri shot her a look of warning. She didn't want anything to take away Danny's joy, especially her friend's negative prophecies concerning this trip. "It will be fine," she assured Margaret with a confidence she didn't feel. "Come on, Danny, let's start loading our supplies."

Danny nodded enthusiastically. As he jumped down from the bunk, his cap fell off, exposing the bald head beneath. Sherri's heart constricted at the visual reminder of the chemo treatments from the weeks before. Although Danny had been a little trouper, Sherri was grateful the treatments were behind them, at least for now.

It took them most of the day to pack the motor home. They had suitcases, boxes and cans of food, lanterns and camping equipment, coats and gloves and anything else they could think of for their home away from home. Danny wasn't satisfied until each and every item was in its place and they were ready to leave the next day.

The packing took longer than expected because they had to explore every nook and cranny. Each cabinet was opened, each drawer pulled out, every built-in convenience was marveled over with appropriate awe.

"I think it's bedtime for you," Sherri said that evening as they finished eating a late supper of soup and grilled-cheese sandwiches. The day had been almost too much for Danny, who'd drooped over the meal and scarcely eaten a bite.

"I'm not tired," Danny protested, although his words lacked conviction. He yawned, his eyelids drooping. "Well, maybe a little," he admitted with a small smile.

"You get ready for bed and I'll come to tuck you in as soon as I clear off these dishes."

Danny nodded, yawning once again as he disappeared down the hallway and into his bedroom. Sherri finished putting the last of their dinner dishes into the dishwasher, then filled the sink with soapy water to wash the pots and pans.

As she worked, her gaze went out the window, to the house next door where the kitchen light burned brightly, illuminating the drapery of darkness that had fallen in the past hour.

Margaret and her husband Jim, and their four boys would probably be at the kitchen table, enjoying the usual noisy, chaotic evening meal. They would all be talking at once, sharing the events of their day.

There were times Sherri envied Margaret her healthy boys and her loving husband, envied with a passion she could almost taste. She envied the noise, the confusion, the love, the family.

Family...she'd dreamed once of a houseful of kids and a handsome husband. But reality was that she and the handsome husband had divorced when Danny was almost four years old. Reality was lonely nights and early mornings of silence. Reality was Danny's illness and living on borrowed time.

"Mom, I'm ready," Danny called from his bedroom.

"Coming," Sherri replied. She dried the last pan and placed it in the appropriate cabinet, then hurried into Danny's bedroom where he awaited their bedtime ritual.

Danny's room was a study in motion. Model airplanes hung suspended on thin wires from the ceiling, their silhouettes dancing in the light from the hallway. Pictures of birds, helicopters and jets decorated every inch of the walls.

From the time Danny was a baby, he'd been fascinated with the action of flight. When he was five, he'd constructed a pair of cardboard wings and tried to fly off the top of the garden shed. The ill-fated landing had resulted in a broken arm and a stern lecture.

Most recently before his illness, he and a buddy had rigged up a bungy-jumping cord to the backyard tree, deciding that bungy jumping was the closest thing to really flying. Thankfully, Sherri had spied the equipment before it could be tested and put to use. Since his illness, there had been no more experiments in actual flying, but Danny's obsession with flight hadn't faded.

Sherri sat on the edge of his bed and stroked the smoothness of his scalp. "Just like when I was a baby, huh?" Danny asked, casting her a sleepy grin.

"Exactly like," she agreed. "Your dad and I thought you'd be bald forever. You didn't have a hint of hair until you were over a year old."

"But I was still the best-looking kid you'd ever seen."

Sherri laughed and touched the end of his nose. "Yes, you were, and now you'd better get right to sleep. We've got a big day tomorrow."

"It's gonna be great, isn't it?" Danny closed his eyes, a sweet smile lingering on his lips. "I can't believe it's really gonna happen. It's gonna be the best time ever."

"Yes," Sherri whispered softly. "It's going to be the best time ever. Are you still sure you don't want any presents?" They would be spending Christmas in the R.V., and so far, Danny had been adamant that the trip alone was present enough for him.

He nodded, his eyes drooping closed once again. "Just us being together is the best Christmas present in the whole wide world."

She pulled the sheet up around his neck and placed a kiss on his forehead. Seeing the soft, even rhythm of his breathing, she stood up and started to leave.

"Mom?"

She turned and looked back at him. With the light from the hallway shining on his features, she was struck by how much he looked like Luke. The strong little chin, the high cheekbones, the sensual bottom lip...a chip off the old block. A bittersweet pang raced through her, there only a moment then gone. "What, honey?"

"It's gonna be just like it used to be. Me and you and Dad all together again like a real family. It's gonna be the best time in my whole life."

Sherri hesitated, then nodded and left the room. She should have told him, she berated herself. She should have told him that there was no way it could ever be the way it used to be. Even though the three of them would be together, there was no way to go back and be a family. Too much time had passed, too many bitter memories made that particular dream of Danny's impossible. She and Luke were divorced and no amount of time spent together would change them into a normal, loving family.

She pulled on her coat and walked out the front door. She sat on the porch swing and pushed her feet against the wood. The motion set the swing moving back and forth in a lulling, easy movement.

Night had fallen completely and insects buzzed and clicked in the darkness. A cold evening breeze rippled through her long dark hair as she continued to swing.

Thank God the weather was cooperating for their winter cross-country trip. The entire country was enjoying an unusually mild winter. She was willing to put up with all the ice and snow Mother Nature might cast their way in a month's time, but she just hoped that for the next three weeks the weather remained moderate.

Leaning her head back, she sighed. She should go to bed. Danny had a big day tomorrow, and so did she. Not only did she want to give Danny the trip of his life, but she also had to figure out how on earth she was going to spend three weeks cooped up in that motor home with Luke.

Luke Morgan threw the last sweatshirt in the duffel bag and zipped it closed. He looked at his wristwatch. Ten minutes until seven. Sherri had said they should be here by seven, so he knew they'd be here any time. Sherri was never late.

He moved the duffel bag by the front door, then plopped down on the bright red futon to wait. He was dreading this trip...knew it was probably the biggest mistake he'd make in his life, and he'd made plenty.

At least he didn't have to worry about anyone watering his plants while he was gone. He looked over in the corner where two dead plants hung in macramé hangers. He sighed and leaned back against the futon.

Sherri. She'd been a closed book in his life. He'd moved on, made a life for himself without her. He was a respected and admired photographer. He was considered a witty and charming date.

Yes, he'd managed to put Sherri in his past quite nicely. They'd worked out agreeable visitation arrangements that included Luke's getting Danny every other weekend he wasn't working. Even with Danny's frequent hospitalizations over the past year, he and Sherri had managed to maintain a healthy distance and civility. They'd worked out their divorce much nicer than they'd managed their marriage.

He looked around the apartment that had been his home for the past year. The futon where he sat and a television set/stereo unit comprised the extent of his furniture.

The walls were covered with some of his best work... pictures of native children in South Africa, fatherless children who were the legacy of the Vietnam era, the despair on young faces in Belfast.

He'd given up his world travels a year ago when Danny had gotten ill, and he now photographed the young, the disillusioned, the hopeless in the United States. That way, he was always no more than a couple hours' plane ride away should Danny need him.

He looked around him again. Sherri would hate this place. Sherri loved order and the one thing his apartment lacked was order. He felt a dull sense of dissatisfaction sweep over him. He really should invest in more furniture, perhaps an end table or two. He eyed the untidy stack of clothing in the corner of the room.

A chest of drawers would be nice . . . maybe a maid could make some sense of his chaos.

He frowned, realizing he was viewing his apartment through her eyes. He pulled himself off the futon and glared out the window. His apartment was fine just the way it was. The futon served as his sofa by day, his bed at night. His clothes were fine in a stack in the corner, as were his magazines, his albums and his photography equipment.

Damn, this trip from hell hadn't even begun yet and already Sherri was an intrusion into his life. He didn't want to go. He couldn't imagine being trapped in an R.V. for three weeks with his ex-wife. He must have been crazy when he'd agreed to the whole thing.

His mind suddenly filled with a vision of Danny. His frown automatically faded, replaced by a small smile. What a kid. He and Sherri might have failed at their marriage, but somehow, the best of both of them had joined together on the night that Danny was conceived. That's why he had agreed to this trip. For Danny.

He stared out the window, seeing a motor home pull to a stop in the parking lot. He looked down at his watch. Bingo . . . seven o'clock on the nose. Some things never changed.

He grabbed his duffel bag, pulled on his jacket, locked the front door, then hurried down to meet them.

Luke felt his heart expand in his chest as Danny stuck his head out the window. "Hi, Dad," he yelled. He opened the door and jumped down from the passenger seat and ran toward Luke. "Hey, big man," Danny said, grinning up at him.

"Hey, little man," Luke replied. He let the duffel bag fall to the concrete and went down to one knee as Danny threw himself into his arms.

For a moment, Luke held him tight, smelling the little-boy scent of him...a scent of sunshine and freedom, of laughter and dreams. Dreams the doctors said would probably not be fulfilled...dreams Luke would sell his soul to see come true.

"Come on, Mom is waiting." Danny wiggled from Luke's tight embrace. He grabbed his father's hand and tugged Luke toward the R.V. "Wait until you see everything inside. It's so awesome. And Mom says if it's not too cold we can make a camp fire every night and toast marshmallows and when we get to the Grand Canyon we're going to rent a helicopter to fly us over it."

"Whoa," Luke said with a laugh. "Slow down. We've got a lot of driving time ahead of us before we get to the Grand Canyon."

"Yeah, but with you and me and Mom all together, it will be fun. We can sing and talk and just be together." Danny tugged impatiently on his father's hand again. "Come on, let's get this show on the road!"

Funny, Luke thought as he stepped into the vehicle. He'd forgotten how small Sherri was...how petite. Sitting behind the steering wheel, clad in a pair of red slacks and a red-and-white-striped long-sleeved blouse, she looked like the cute little teenager he had fallen in love with years before.

He had a sudden vision of the way she had looked on the day they had gotten married. It hadn't been much of a ceremony, a simple civil service in city hall. She'd been eighteen years old and had gazed up at him as if he were her entire world. It wasn't until they'd been married several months that he'd realized he *was* her entire world.

"Hi," he said awkwardly.

She smiled a greeting, her big brown eyes narrowing slightly as she looked at his duffel bag. "Is that all your luggage?"

He nodded. "I travel light." He saw her lips compress in disapproval, as if she knew he'd thrown together clothes in the bag only moments before, which of course he had.

"I'll take it, Dad. I'll store it with ours," Danny said, taking the bag from him. He disappeared into the back as Sherri started the engine.

"You want me to drive?" he asked with a touch of irritation. She'd probably packed a month ago... sixteen suitcases full of useless items.

"I'll drive until I get tired, then you can take over," she answered, her voice pleasant, but distant.

Luke settled into the seat with a sigh. He stared out the window at the passing scenery, waiting for her to say something, anything to ease the awkward silence that grew and expanded with each passing moment.

What do you say to the woman you'd been married to for five years, and divorced from for the past five? he wondered. He could tell her about his date last Friday night, but he had a feeling she wouldn't want to hear about it. Besides, it had been a horrible night and he was doing his best to forget it. He could tell her about his latest photography assignment, but she'd always resented his work.

They'd had little in common years ago. After five years of separation, he suspected that hadn't changed. Maybe it was best that he just keep his mouth shut.

He sighed again. He leaned forward and turned on the radio, relaxing somewhat as the sounds of an old rock and roll song filled the motor home.

"Uh...would you mind leaving it off until we get out of this rush-hour traffic?" she asked politely.

"Okay," he agreed reluctantly. He turned it off, remembering that she'd never liked to drive with the radio playing.

He was aware of Danny returning from the back and sitting down in the chair just behind him. Danny leaned forward and placed a hand on Luke's arm, and his other hand on Sherri's shoulder. "This is gonna be so much fun," he exclaimed with all the excitement a nine-year-old could generate. "We're going to have the greatest time in the world, aren't we?" His words were met with silence. "Aren't we?" he prompted, squeezing Luke's arm.

"Sure, the greatest," Luke replied faintly.

"The best," Sherri added. She looked at Luke, and in her eyes he saw the same dull dread he knew was in his own.

He smiled weakly, then turned his gaze out the window. Yes, this was definitely going to be the trip from hell.

Chapter Two

Sherri feigned sleep and studied Luke beneath her lowered lashes. She'd spent the last six hours driving and after they'd stopped for lunch, had relinquished control of the vehicle to him.

She'd spent the past five years trying not to really look at him whenever they happened to run into each other. She now took the opportunity to examine the man she had once been married to, the man she had once loved above all else.

Luke had always been handsome. Sherri was honest enough to know that it had been his intense good looks that had initially attracted her to him.

He was still sinfully attractive. The passage of time had merely intensified his bold features. His chin was square and strong, his nose a Roman feature. He's wearing his dark hair longer, she observed. She liked it. She decided it gave him a rakish look that complemented his devil-may-care personality.

He'd taken off the leather bomber jacket he'd been wearing this morning and was clad in a short-sleeved T-shirt that exposed his firmly muscled, tanned arms. He had the body of a man who worked out, but she knew Luke was too undisciplined to follow any regular workout regimen.

She looked at his hands, gripping the steering wheel competently. She'd always loved his hands. They were artist hands, slender and long-fingered, yet masculine with the dark curly hair that dotted each knuckle.

He talked with his hands, gesturing often as if they were an extension of his thought processes. They used to laugh about it. She'd teased that if his hands were tied behind his back, he would be completely tonguetied.

"Sherri?"

His voice caused her to squeeze her eyes more tightly closed. She didn't want him to know that she'd been looking at him. She kept her breathing even and rhythmic, feigning deep slumber.

"I know you aren't sleeping, Sherri." His voice was softly indulgent and she could hear the smile in it.

She cracked an eyelid. "How do you know I'm not?" she asked, suddenly irritable.

"Because you always sleep with your mouth hanging open," he observed.

She sat up straighter in the seat. "I most certainly do not," she replied stiffly.

He smiled, a smirking, knowing grin that instantly fueled her unreasonable aggravation with him. "For the five years we were married, you never, ever slept with your mouth closed."

"Well, it's been a long time since you've slept with me and nobody else has ever complained," she snapped. She groaned inwardly. Now why had she said that? In the years since her divorce from Luke, there had been no opportunity for anyone to complain about her sleeping habits. Other than the occasional night when Danny had a nightmare and had needed some assurance, she'd slept alone.

"We need to talk," he said, not taking his gaze off the highway they traveled.

"Talk about what?" She sat up in the seat and eyed him curiously.

"About the silence we've suffered through for the last six hours."

"It hasn't been silent...Danny has been chattering." Sherri turned around in her seat, looking for her son.

"Don't worry," Luke said. "He went back a little while ago to take a nap. He can't hear us." He looked at her for a moment, then redirected his gaze to the road. "Sherri, I don't know about you, but so far this trip has been damned uncomfortable. The tension between us is so ripe, Danny can't help but feel it. We can't have the whole trip like this."

Sherri thought about those six hours. She had driven, Luke had stared out the window and Danny had talked. It had been the inane chatter of a kid who sensed tension and was attempting to dispel it. "So, what do you suggest?" she asked.

"I don't know. All I do know is that we've got three weeks of close contact, intimate togetherness and a Christmas holiday to get through. For the sake of that kid back there, we'd better be able to put our past behind us and act like reasonable adults."

"I can do whatever it takes to make Danny happy," she answered.

Luke grinned. "I think it would make Danny happy if you tried to be nice to me."

Sherri glared at him in outrage. Was he somehow trying to take advantage of this whole situation? It would be just like him to do that. She instantly steadied herself. Of course he wasn't. He didn't want to be with her any more than she wanted to be with him. He was merely thinking of Danny. And she would do the same. "I can be nice to you . . . for Danny's sake."

"Okay, then it's agreed. For Danny's sake, we'll act like we really like each other."

Sherri grimaced. "I don't know if I'm that talented an actress," she muttered.

"You are, I can still remember all those times you acted like you enjoyed my lovemaking."

"Oh!" Sherri gasped at his temerity. She sputtered for a moment, opening and closing her mouth in an effort to find effectively scathing words. When nothing strong enough came to mind, she turned around in the seat, staring out the passenger window and studiously ignoring the soft chuckle he emitted.

Why did he have to mention that? she thought. Of all the things that had happened between them, of all the memories both good and bad she had entertained in the past, their lovemaking was something she'd never looked back on. That had been one particular set of memories she'd refused to acknowledge, refused to indulge herself in remembering.

But now the memories exploded in her mind, reminding her of the intensity, the wonder of sexual fulfillment she had always found in his arms. He'd been her first...her only. Sex had been their common ground, the only thing they had really done well together. It was what had kept their marriage alive much longer than it should have been.

She squeezed her eyes tightly closed, refusing to give those vivid memories any substance, shoving the disturbing visions firmly out of her mind.

As the motor home traveled onward, she allowed the motion to lull her to sleep.

Luke glanced over at Sherri and realized this time she really was sound asleep. A small smile curved his lips upward as he saw that her mouth hung slightly agape. Yes, she was definitely asleep.

He relaxed his grip on the steering wheel and reached over and flipped on the radio, turning it up so he could hear it, but not so loud it would intrude on Sherri's slumber. The last thing he wanted to do was wake her up. One thing he remembered quite well, a tired Sherri was a cranky Sherri. His grin widened. The first thing he'd learned about her after marriage

was that when she was tired her nose itched, and when
he saw her scratching the tip of her pert little nose, he
knew to watch out and give her a wide berth.

He eyed her again, humming along to Elvis's
crooning 'Love Me Tender.' He didn't know why he
had thrown out that comment about their lovemaking, but somehow he knew it had been because of a
perverse wish to shake her up, watch her blush.

She'd always been so damned tight, so rigid. She'd
come to him with a full structured set of ideals on love
and marriage, ideals that no man would have been
able to live up to... especially him.

He'd wondered how many others had tried. No
complaints, she'd said and he'd been surprised to feel
a swift, strong shaft of jealousy sweep through him.
He'd thought he'd gotten beyond that particular
emotion long ago where she was concerned.

He shook his head ruefully. He hadn't exactly been
a monk since their divorce. He'd just never thought
about Sherri's being with somebody else. He'd never
contemplated the thought of her breathing her sweet
sighs of passion into the hollow of another man's
neck. He'd never considered that another man's hands
might stroke the smoothness of her shapely legs, caress the satiny texture of her breasts. He now realized
it had been the height of conceit to assume that Sherri
would never love another... never make love to another man.

He looked at her again, this time studying her in her
vulnerable state of sleep. She'd done something different to her hair. Although she still wore it long, be-

low her shoulders, the rich darkness was now shot through with strands of lighter shades. He liked it, he decided. It gave her a softer, more stylish look.

He could smell her, a curious mingling of floral perfume and that indefinable scent that had always belonged to her alone. He'd often boasted that in a roomful of women, blindfolded he would be able to pick out Sherri by her scent. It had always turned him on. He was shocked to realize it was having that same kind of effect on him now.

With an edge of irritation, he cracked open the window, allowing in the cold December air, needing it to banish the heat that suddenly flooded through his veins.

He jumped as Danny touched him on the shoulder. "Hi, sport, have a good nap?" he asked, relieved for the distraction from his crazy thoughts.

Danny nodded. "How long has Mom been asleep?" he asked.

"Not long," Luke answered, then grinned. "I see she still sleeps with her mouth open."

Danny laughed. "Yeah, last Easter Sunday I woke her up by dropping a black jelly bean between her lips. Boy, did she get mad."

"I can imagine," Luke replied. "She always did hate black licorice," he added, making Danny laugh again.

"Where are we?" Danny asked, peering out the side window.

"About an hour from our first campsite. According to your mother's schedule, we're stopping at a place just outside Akron, Ohio, for tonight."

"Cool, I've never been to Ohio before," Danny observed.

"You've never been out of Connecticut before," Luke reminded his son. "Are you getting hungry?"

"Not really. What about you?"

"Yes, I'm starting to get hungry," Luke replied.

"Mom made out menus for each night. Hang on and I'll tell you what she's cooking tonight." Danny scurried out of his seat and rummaged around in one of the drawers.

Menus. Of course, Sherri would make menus, Luke thought. And lists. There was probably a list detailing all the lists she had made for the trip.

"Steaks and baked potatoes. Sounds good, huh," Danny exclaimed, sitting back down behind Luke.

"Sounds terrific," Luke agreed.

"You think we'll be able to have a camp fire and cook the steaks outside?" Danny asked.

"We'll have to wait and see what sort of campsite we stop at," Luke explained. "If it's too cold out and we can't have a fire, then we'll be eating in."

"Okay," Danny agreed easily.

Luke's heart swelled with pride, and the peculiar kind of dread that was always there when he thought of his son. The latest prognosis was that Danny had six months to a year to live. There had been a time when Luke had been unable to imagine a life with a son. Now he couldn't imagine life without Danny.

"Hey, Dad?"

"Yeah, sport?" Luke shoved his dark thoughts away.

"I told Mom I wanted to sleep on the top bunk, but she said we'd have to see. So what do you think? Can I have the top bunk and you and Mom can share the bottom one?"

Amusement rippled through Luke at the very thought. He tried to imagine he and Sherri in the small confines of the lower bunk. It was an interesting image.

Of course, it would be only natural that they'd inadvertently touch each other. A rubbing of shoulders, a brush of a thigh...it could be quite stimulating. But it was a stimulation neither of them needed, or wanted, he reminded himself firmly. Besides, if Sherri got cranky when she was tired, he'd hate to see her if she realized she would be sharing a bed with him once again.

"How about us men take the top one?" he countered. "If we can share my futon on weekends, surely we can share the upper bunk for the duration of this trip."

"Okay," Danny replied. Luke expelled a sigh. One crisis averted. He wondered how many more lay in wait for him.

Sherri awoke as the motor home pulled to a halt. "Where are we?" she asked, sitting up and looking out the window for orientation.

"At the Happy Camper's Park just outside of Akron." Luke shut off the engine and opened his door. "Just sit tight and I'll get us a parking space for the night."

"I'll come with you, okay, big man?" Danny asked, scrambling after him.

"Okay, little man," Luke replied.

"Danny, your coat!" Sherri called, holding the winter jacket out to him. She didn't care if Luke caught a cold, but she didn't want Danny getting ill. He shrugged on the jacket and together he and Luke left the R.V.

Sherri watched as the two of them approached the office. Her heart constricted as Luke threw an arm around Danny's shoulders. They walked so much alike, with a sort of jaunty, rambling roll of natural arrogance. In Luke it was incredibly sexy, in Danny it was just plain cute.

As they disappeared into the office, she got up out of her seat and began putting together the items for their dinner. One thing she couldn't take away from Luke: he was a terrific father. Even when he'd been traveling and was out of the country, a week didn't pass that Danny didn't receive several letters from wherever Luke was working.

It had surprised her over the years, the commitment that Luke had made to his son. She'd always believed the only thing Luke could be committed to was his work and his need for excitement. That had certainly always come before his commitment to her. She shoved the bitterness aside, knowing it would ruin the taste of the steaks.

Besides, it was the past, and there was no way to change it, no way to go back and reclaim it. She didn't need Luke anymore. The only thing she needed was to make sure this was the best three weeks of Danny's life.

"We're all set," Luke said as he climbed into the driver's seat. "We'll have electrical and water hookups." He restarted the motor home.

"And the man says we can have a camp fire so we can cook our steaks outside," Danny said with excitement. "We can toast marshmallows, then tell ghost stories and stuff."

"Sounds like a winner to me," Sherri replied.

It took them nearly an hour to hook up and get a fire burning. By the time they cooked the steaks and ate, darkness had fallen and the air held a sharper nip of winter. The fire provided a welcoming light and warmth against the night. Again, Sherri was thankful that the weather was cooperating by remaining unusually mild for December. Now, if it would just hold.

She settled back against the fallen tree limb that provided her a seat in front of the fire. A quiet contentment swept through her as she listened to Luke and Danny talk about sports.

The dinner conversation had been pleasant. They had talked about the weather, their travel plans for the next day, the campsite...they'd managed to find things to talk about that were nonthreatening and safe.

Now if they could just continue in the same vein for the next three weeks....

She gazed across the fire, watching her son's face as he animatedly dissected the last New York Yankees ball game with Luke. She smiled, seeing her son's hands flail in the air as he described a particular pop fly. Definitely a chip off the old block.

In the glow of the fire, Danny's face looked like a youthful miniature of his father's. But according to the doctors, his face would never reach the maturity of Luke's. Sherri shoved this thought aside, unable to deal with the grief, the breath-stealing pain that tore through her at thoughts of losing Danny.

Doctors have been known to be wrong, she reminded herself firmly. And miracles did still happen in this world. All she had to do was keep praying for their own special miracle.

Her heart expanded as she heard Danny's lilting laughter, saw Luke's responding grin. She focused on their conversation, realizing that their talk had turned from sports to ghost stories.

As Luke related to Danny a story he'd heard while in Ireland, Sherri got up and went into the camper. Opening one of the cabinets, she drew out her camera. She wanted to chronicle this trip, these memories. She'd been surprised that Luke hadn't brought his camera equipment. During their marriage, he'd even carried it with him on short trips to the grocery store, afraid he might miss the opportunity of getting an award-winning photo.

She loaded the film and checked the batteries to make sure the flash would work, then went outside and sat across from the two males.

Luke was at the climax of his story, his voice low and creepy. Danny's eyes were wide, his mouth opened in an ohh of anticipation. Sherri snapped a picture, laughing as the flash made Danny jump and yell in surprise.

"Mom, you scared me," he exclaimed. He clasped a hand to his heart and grinned. "Hey, let me take one of you and Dad," he urged suddenly.

"Oh, no," Sherri protested, looking to Luke for support.

"Come on, Mom, just one," Danny pressed, his big blue eyes pleading his cause.

It's just a picture, Sherri told herself as she reluctantly gave Danny the camera. But there was something intimate about a photograph, an image that lasted despite time and change. Luke had always told her that he thought pictures were the most telling medium of all, that relationships, character and emotion could all be read by studying a photo.

As she moved to sit next to Luke, she wondered what perceptions people would draw years from now about the picture of the man and woman sitting by the camp fire. Would they know the two were divorced, or would they guess that they were lovers enjoying a camp-out?

She eased down next to Luke, immediately able to smell his scent, a heady combination of spicy cologne and wood smoke and the smell of worn leather from his bomber jacket. She held herself stiff, not touching him, but aware of his body heat warming her as effectively as the flames of the fire.

"Relax," Luke murmured to her as Danny worked the focus. "Give the kid what he wants." He placed his arm around her shoulder and pulled her close against his side.

"That's great," Danny exclaimed in delight.

In the moment it took for him to snap the picture, myriad emotions flooded through Sherri. She had spent the last five years trying to forget everything about Luke, yet in the single instant in his arms, her body remembered the sweet familiarity of his touch.

The second the flash went off, with white dots still dancing in front of her eyes, she jerked away from Luke's touch and stood up. "That's enough pictures for one night," she said as she took the camera back from Danny. "I think I'll go in and take a quick shower."

Luke grinned, his gray-blue eyes lingering on her for a moment. "While you shower, Danny and I will put out the fire."

With a curt nod, Sherri hurried into the motor home. The shower was a confounded contraption. The nozzle produced a pathetic spray of water that was virtually ineffective against banishing the lingering feel of Luke's body pressed against her side.

It had shocked her, the momentary stab of desire that had suddenly reared its head when he'd pressed her against his side. It was an emotion she hadn't felt for a very long time, had thought never to feel again.

"Ridiculous," she scoffed aloud, scrubbing her skin to a rosy hue with the washcloth and fresh-scented bar of soap. It had been shock she'd felt, not desire. It had been surprise and distaste. After all, how could she possibly feel desire for a man she disliked? How could she feel desire for a man who'd taken her love and left her bitter and empty? It had been a long time since she'd felt a man's arms surrounding her, her body had simply reacted to the novelty of the embrace, nothing more.

By the time she'd finished showering and changed into a long, demure sleep shirt, Danny and Luke were back inside. They sat at the table, sharing a bedtime snack of peanut-butter crackers and milk.

"Danny, when you're finished there, take your shower and don't forget to brush your teeth," Sherri reminded him.

"Ah, Mom, we're on vacation," Danny protested.

"Hey, sport, dirt and cavities don't take vacations," Luke said firmly. He stood up and put away the crackers and milk. "Besides, I don't want a stinky, tooth-decayed bunk mate."

"Okay." Danny laughed and headed for the shower.

When he was gone, Sherri busied herself wiping the table and counters, conscious of Luke's gaze following her movements. "You're staring," she finally said as she sat down across from him.

"Yes, I am," he agreed with a lazy smile. "I was just observing the fact that you look good. I like what you've done to your hair."

She ran a hand through it self-consciously. "Thanks."

"Since our divorce, you've only managed to get more attractive."

She flushed. "What did you expect? That without you in my life, I'd somehow fall apart?"

"It would have done my ego wonders if you had." The lazy grin widened.

"Gosh, Luke, I'm really sorry that I couldn't accommodate your massive ego, but I've not only survived since our divorce, I've actually thrived." She tilted her chin upward, returning his gaze with an edge of defiance. She studiously shoved aside the memory of how frightened she had once been that she wouldn't survive, that she would fall apart without him.

He stretched out his long jean-clad legs and grinned at her. "I've managed to do pretty well myself since our divorce," he said. "I'm considered quite a catch in the circles I travel."

Sherri smiled thinly. "I'm sure you have to beat the women off with sticks since you're such a sexy hunk."

"You really think so?" His dark eyebrows danced upward.

"Hmm, I'm sure you have to carry two baseball bats with you to fend off the attention of love-starved females," she replied sarcastically.

"No, I meant do you really think I'm a sexy hunk?" He leaned up over the table, so close she could feel his warm breath on her face, see something unfathomable in his eyes. He reached out and traced the swell of her bottom lip with a fingertip. "You know, Danny wanted to sleep in the top bunk all by himself. You and I could share the bottom one . . . share a little passion for old times' sake. What do you think?''

Sherri reeled back in the chair but before she could scald him with a flurry of scathing words, Danny stepped out of the bathroom. "All done," he exclaimed.

"Terrific, I'll tuck you in." Sherri escaped Luke's proximity, following her son back into the sleeping area. "Make sure you leave plenty of room for your father," she said loudly enough for Luke to hear.

"I think I'll take a quick shower," Luke said, his voice still filled with the lazy amusement that only fueled Sherri's irritation with him.

"Danny and I will just go on to bed," she replied coolly.

As he disappeared into the bathroom, Sherri gave her son a kiss, then crawled beneath the sheets on the lower bunk.

The nerve of the man, she fumed inwardly. She punched her pillow and flopped over on her side. He'd been playing with her, using his overt sensuality to get to her. How many of their fights had ended with him cajoling her into bed, sweet-talking her out of her anger and into his arms? Share a little passion for old times' sake . . . oh, the nerve of him!

Luke and his lazy, sexy charm. It had always been coupled with a touch of arrogance that had merely increased its potency. His arrogance didn't cross the line into conceit. If it did, it wouldn't be so damned appealing. She punched her pillow once again.

"The beds are kinda hard, aren't they?" Danny said from above her.

"A little," she replied, but she knew it wasn't the physical discomfort of the bed that bothered her. It was the fact that she still found Luke sexy. After all these years, she still found his naughty charm stimulating. Damn his handsome hide!

She jumped as above the sounds of the water running in the shower, she heard him begin to sing. Luke had always sang in the shower... always sang loudly and badly.

Some things never change, she thought as she heard him lustily singing the words to a familiar Garth Brooks tune. Without the words, the song would have been totally unrecognizable.

Danny's giggles filled the air. His laughter grew stronger as Luke's singing became louder. The sound of her son's laughter fed a sudden spurt of her own.

"He really is bad, isn't he, Mom?" Danny said amid fits of giggling.

"He is," Sherri agreed. "And the frightening part is he honestly doesn't know how bad he is." Again, Danny and Sherri burst into laughter.

They were still giggling when Luke finally stepped out of the bathroom. "What's so funny?" he asked.

Sherri's laughter died instantly on her lips as she stared at him. He stood backlit by the light from the bathroom. He was clad only in a pair of boxer shorts, exposing his firm muscular chest, flat abdomen and long masculine legs. "Nothing," she murmured. She quickly turned over on her other side, facing the wall, closing her eyes against the vision that was momentarily burned into her brain. They were silk boxers, bright red and incredibly sexy. Drat the man, anyway, she fumed.

She was vaguely aware of him turning out all the lights and pulling himself up into the bunk above her. She sensed the mattress depressing beneath his weight, smelled the clean soapy scent that emanated from him. She squeezed her eyes more tightly closed. Margaret had been right. This whole idea was a study in insanity.

"Sweet dreams, Sherri," Luke murmured, his voice softly mocking as if he knew the view of his scantily clad body had disturbed her.

She grunted in response and punched her pillow a final time. She'd forgotten how potent Luke's sexuality was, how overtly male he was. She hadn't considered her own vulnerability, the fact that she had been without male companionship for too long, that her body remembered Luke's caresses, his lovemaking far too keenly for sanity's sake.

I just have to concentrate on all the things I don't like about him, she thought. Aside from the failure of their marriage, she had to hang on to the little things that drove her crazy. He ate ketchup on his steak. He was tone-deaf and loved to sing. He popped his knuckles to see her squirm.

As she slowly drifted off to sleep, she remembered something else she hated about him. He snored.

Chapter Three

Luke awoke first. The dawn light illuminated the interior of the motor home with a golden glow, and outside a bird chirped softly, as if welcoming the coming morning light.

He knew he should get up, get the utilities unhooked so they would be ready to roll when Sherri and Danny awakened. But he didn't move. Instead, he remained still, drinking in the sensations that surrounded him.

Although the bed was little more than a thin foam pad covering plywood, and the ceiling was suffocatingly close to his nose, he couldn't remember the last time he'd been so comfortable, so content.

Danny's warmth pressed sweetly against him and he could hear Sherri's soft breaths as she slept soundly below. He'd forgotten what it was like to wake up and listen to the sounds of somebody else's sleep. The women he'd dated, the ones he'd made love to since his divorce, had never been allowed to spend the night. That was an intimacy he shared with nobody.

He rolled over on his side and peeked into the bunk below, staring at the woman who'd once been his wife. A smile curved his lips as he saw her mouth hanging slightly open. It was a pretty mouth, eminently feminine and dainty. Her lashes were long and dark enough so she rarely wore mascara. Her hair was a dark spill of brown and gold against the pristine white of the pillowcase. She was curled up on her side, her hands clasped beneath her cheek. She looked soft and touchable.

His smile widened into a full-fledged grin as he rolled over onto his back, imagining how quickly soft and touchable would become prickly and hateful if he were to crawl into bed with her. And yet there was a certain appeal in the thought of making love to her again. Sex had always been terrific with Sherri. She was a giving lover, eager to please as well as be pleased. Had they managed to stay in bed twenty-four hours a day, then perhaps they'd never have divorced.

One more time for old times' sake...he didn't know why he had said that to her the night before. He'd known before the words had left his mouth that they would make her mad. Yet, she'd always managed to evoke in him a strange perverse need to shake her up, and sex had always been the way to do it.

When he'd seen her in that sleep shirt the night before, it had brought back memories...disturbing ones that instantly threatened. She'd always worn cotton nightshirts to bed. He could still remember the lemony sunshine scent of them, the way the cotton would warm with her body heat. He could remember the texture of the material stretched taut across her nipples as he caressed her breasts.

Yes, somehow he'd found her threatening, and he'd responded to the threat by saying things he knew would make her angry. The last thing they needed from each other was a casual, physical fling.

He released a small sigh and flung an arm over his eyes, thinking over their brief conversation from the night before. In truth, when they'd divorced, he had been surprised that she hadn't fallen apart. There had been a small part of him that had expected it, anticipated it.

He'd been surprised at the strength and determination she'd shown in wanting to make it entirely on her own. She had wanted no alimony and only a small amount of child support. She'd insisted they sell the house and split the equity. The only thing she'd requested was that he help her obtain loans so she could go to college and get a teaching degree. Too bad that it had taken the divorce for her to show him the strength he'd desperately longed to see in her during their marriage.

Oh well, water under the bridge now. Shoving aside the past, Luke eased himself off the top bunk and to the floor, landing silently, with the grace of a large cat. Casting one last look at his sleeping son and ex-wife, he yanked on a pair of jeans and his bomber jacket, then went outside to get the motor home ready to travel once again.

Sherri was up and had coffee made when he came back in. "Good morning," he said cheerfully, shrugging out of his jacket.

"'Mornin'," she muttered, scratching the tip of her nose with two fingers. "Where's your shirt?" she asked, frowning as she stared at his bare chest.

Uh-oh, Luke thought, remembering the warning signs. She apparently hadn't slept as well as he had. "Hmm, that coffee smells terrific." He was determined to remain cheerful. "You want me to pour you a cup?" he offered.

She nodded and sat down at the table, stifling a yawn with the back of her hand. She once again scratched the tip of her nose as he set the cup of coffee before her. "I need about a pot of this to get me started this morning."

"Didn't sleep well?"

"Those beds aren't meant for sleeping. They're torture devices." Her brown eyes raked him irritably. "And I'd forgotten all about your snoring."

"Sorry," he replied with a shrug. He grinned at her, knowing he was a fool, but enjoying it. "You know in the past what always stopped my snoring..."

He saw the blush of memory darken her cheeks and knew she was remembering that they used to laugh because the only nights Luke didn't snore were on the nights they made love.

"Stuffing a sock in your mouth would have the same effect," she said dryly, then took another sip of her coffee.

Luke laughed, reared back in his chair and studied her. She was so familiar... and yet so different from what he remembered. She was like an old song with new harmony, different pitches and notes. "Do you like teaching?" he asked suddenly, realizing he knew next to nothing about her life, her work. "What is it? Third grade?"

"Second, and I love it." She smiled, her brown eyes softening to the color of melted caramels. "As far as I'm concerned, second-graders are the best. They're old enough to be manageable, yet young enough to truly believe that the teacher knows everything." She smiled her pleasure. Luke again noticed how pretty she looked. The morning sunshine was just beginning to streak into the window and caressed her delicate features. "It's a wonderful job, teaching children. I love my work."

She gazed at him, her eyes seeming to pierce through his skin, into his soul. "I'm surprised you didn't bring your camera equipment with you. There was a time when I thought it was permanently mounted on your hand."

Luke got up and poured himself another cup of coffee, unsure how to answer her, unsure himself why the thought of bringing the camera along on this particular trip had been abhorrent. "I just didn't feel like it," he finally replied. "I wanted this to be pure pleasure, not work."

"I always thought for you they were one and the same," she observed.

Although there was no censure in her voice, the words rankled, felt like a criticism. "Maybe you aren't the only one who's changed in the last five years," he answered curtly. He sat down at the table and stared out the window for a long moment. "It's going to be a gorgeous day. Cold, but lots of sunshine. I hope this weather keeps up for the remainder of the trip."

She nodded and he saw the tiny flicker of pain that darkened her eyes as she gazed toward the back where Danny still slept. He knew what she was thinking...how many more gorgeous mornings would Danny have to enjoy? How many more days would he feel like getting out of bed?

"He's too thin," he said gruffly. "We need to fatten him up on this trip."

"He doesn't have much of an appetite," Sherri explained. "I try to entice him with his favorite foods as often as possible."

"How is he ever going to become a world-class jet pilot if he doesn't have a little more meat on his bones?" he returned. She looked at him, her eyes bottomless pits of despair. She knew that Danny would never grow up to be a world-class jet pilot. Deep inside, Luke knew it, too.

He stood up suddenly, unable to acknowledge her pain, knowing that in doing so he would release some of the pain that he constantly shoved away. He couldn't face it, not now, not yet. "Let's get this show on the road. We want to be able to make St. Louis by tonight.''

"Whew, I'm stuffed," Danny exclaimed, his mouth still exhibiting the sticky remains of several roasted marshmallows.

They had made good time all day and were now parked in a small campsite outside St. Louis, Missouri. They'd just finished a meal of hot dogs and potato chips, topped off by marshmallows blackened by the fire's flame.

The day had gone well. Luke had been on good behavior, keeping the conversation pleasant yet nonpersonal enough to be comfortable. They'd sung one song after another to pass the time, then played license-plate bingo for a couple of hours.

Danny's eyes had shone with happiness throughout the day, his excitement peaking when they'd stopped in a gift shop and he'd found a new model airplane he didn't have.

Sherri cleared away the last of the food and put it inside the camper, then returned to the fire's edge, where Luke and Danny's conversation had drifted to childhood memories.

"I got my first camera when I was just about your age," Luke said. "And after my first roll of film, I knew what I wanted to do with the rest of my life." Luke chuckled, a deep rich sound that filled the night. "I drove my parents crazy, posing them, sneaking up on them with my camera, taking their pictures over and over again."

"I remember you taking lots of pictures of me and Mom when I was little," Danny said.

"He was a picture-taking guerrilla soldier, lying in wait every time we turned around," Sherri exclaimed with a laugh. "It got so I was afraid to take a bath or a shower for fear he'd be lurking in the room with his infernal camera." She moved closer to the fire, enjoying the warmth that emanated from the flames.

"Ah, but I've got some great memories captured on celluloid," Luke reminded her.

"I've got lots of good memories," Danny told them.

Luke laughed indulgently and rubbed his knuckles across Danny's head. "It's easy to have memories when you're nine years old. You don't have that many years to remember."

Danny playfully punched his dad in the side, then leaned into him and sighed with contentment. "I remember lots of good things. You know what I remember most of all?"

"What's that?" Sherri asked, enjoying the picture of the little boy leaning into the man. Luke's arm was thrown around Danny's thin back and his hand rubbed against Danny's coat in the stroking motion of love.

"Sunday mornings," Danny answered.

Sherri looked at him in surprise. "Sunday mornings? What was so special about them?"

Danny smiled softly, his eyes reflecting the pleasure of his memory. "When I was little and I'd wake up on Sunday mornings, you and Dad would still be in bed. Dad would be reading the paper and drinking coffee, and you'd be sleeping next to him. I'd run to the bed and jump in between you and you'd both snuggle me under the blankets and it just felt so good, you know? I just felt all safe and warm."

Sherri nodded slowly, her son's words bringing back in vivid detail memory of those lazy Sunday mornings. The smell of Luke's coffee...the soft rustle as he turned the pages of the newspaper...Danny's little body snuggled warmly against her side...special moments frozen in time, moments she'd forgotten about until this very moment.

She looked at Luke across the fire, noting the way the flickering light illuminated the strength of his jawline, the darker shades of his five o'clock shadow, the dark hair that fell carelessly across his forehead. She remembered other things about Sunday mornings.

When Luke finished reading the paper, he'd wrestle with Danny for a few minutes, then send him into the living room to watch cartoons. After Danny left, he'd close their bedroom door and make slow languid love to her.

She stared at him across the fire's glow, remembering those moments of intimacy in the cocoon of warm sheets. Her neck tingled as she replayed the way his lips felt nibbling evocatively on her skin. Did he still utter those low sighs that had once sent chills of pleasure up her spine? Would her breasts still fit so perfectly into the warmth of his hands?

A slow burning blush crept across her cheeks and a responding grin of knowledge curved Luke's lips. She felt the blush intensifying and stifled the impulse to throw her coffee mug at his smirking face. Drat the man, anyway. Those were memories better left alone.

"Dad, tell me more about when you were a little boy," Danny urged, gazing up at his father with adoring eyes.

"Let me see..." Luke frowned, as if working hard to remember. "I rode a friendly dinosaur to school and wrote all my assignments on stone tablets."

"Dad!" Danny giggled and elbowed Luke in the stomach. "Tell me about when you were in Africa."

As Luke told Danny of his travels abroad, Sherri watched her son's face, loving the expressive twinkle in his eyes, so like his father's. Danny was a bundle of curiosity and loved to hear about the faraway places Luke had been, places Danny would probably never see. Sherri shivered, shoving away this thought and refocusing on their conversation.

"Now tell me about when you first met Mom," Danny said, grinning at Sherri across the dancing flames.

Luke's gaze met Sherri's across the fire's glow. He smiled, not the usual smirking grin, but the soft smile of remembrance. "Ah, yes, I was working as a freelance photographer on the local newspaper and they sent me to the local high school to take a picture of some brain kid who'd just won a full scholarship to Yale. I didn't want to go. I was twenty-one years old and full of myself and didn't want to have to spend any time at all with those immature babies at the high school.''

''But you went, anyway,'' Danny said.

''Sure, it was my job and I had to.'' Luke stretched out his long, lean legs, his smile widening as his gaze stayed fixed on Sherri's face. ''So there I was, taking pictures of this brainchild in the courtyard and I turned around and there was your mother peering out the window.''

Sherri felt her heart expand, filled with thoughts of that moment in time. She'd stood at the window for some time, watching the sexy photographer in the tight jeans, admiring the broadness of his shoulders, his cute rear end. She could still remember that moment when he'd turned around and their gazes had locked. When that slow, sexy grin had lifted the corners of his mouth, she knew she was lost. She had fallen hard, in the space of a second, in love with Luke.

''So, what did she look like?'' Danny pressed Luke to continue.

''Oh, she was so ugly! She was cross-eyed and had a wart on the end of her nose,'' Luke teased, earning him another punch in the side from his son.

''She could never be ugly,'' Danny protested. ''Tell me what she looked like.''

Again a soft smile curved Luke's lips, and Sherri felt a responding warmth curl inside her stomach. ''She was wearing a bright red dress with blue flowers on it and her hair was pulled back in a messy bundle and I thought she was the most gorgeous little thing I'd ever seen.''

"The dress was blue with red diamonds and my hair was in a ponytail," Sherri corrected. He never managed to remember it right.

"That really doesn't matter," Danny insisted. "What matters is that he saw you and he thought you were pretty. She's still pretty, isn't she, Dad?"

Luke's gaze lingered on her for a long moment, then he nodded. "Yes, she's still pretty," he agreed in a hushed voice.

"And what did you think of Dad?" Danny asked her.

"She thought I was gorgeous," Luke quipped.

"I thought he was the most obnoxious man I'd ever met," Sherri said honestly. Danny laughed as Luke groaned.

"But cute," Luke added with a grin.

Sherri hesitated, then laughed. "Yes, and cute," she admitted.

"And you dated and fell in love and got married." Danny smiled, the smile slowly shifting into a perplexed frown. "So how come you guys got divorced?" he asked, looking at them both curiously.

"He was impossible to live with."

"She was a pain to live with."

They spoke at the same time, then laughed self-consciously. "Danny, we were very young when we got married," Sherri continued, her gaze consciously focused away from Luke. "I had just turned eighteen and your dad was only twenty-two. We didn't really know what marriage was all about. We wanted different things from life, needed more than the other could give."

"But you loved each other," Danny protested, obviously trying to understand the complicated world of adults and relationships.

Luke looked helplessly at Sherri. "Sometimes love just isn't enough," she finally responded, knowing her answer was inadequate, but unable to expand any further. She stood up and set her coffee mug down. "And now, my little man, it's bedtime."

"Ah, Mom," Danny protested.

"Better hit the hay, Danny. Tomorrow we've got that stop at the Indian reservation. You don't want to be too tired," Luke reminded him. "Besides, the fire is going out and when it does, it will be too cold for us out here."

Reluctantly, Danny nodded and stood up. It took Sherri only a few minutes to tuck him in, then she went back to where Luke still sat by the fire. "He wants you to go inside and kiss him good-night," she said.

Luke stood and started to go inside, but paused at the door. "You want me to bring you more coffee when I come out?"

"Okay, thanks," she agreed, reluctant to leave the fire's edge and go in.

Luke grabbed her cup and disappeared into the motor home. When he was gone, Sherri leaned back and released a small sigh. She was grateful that the reminiscing was over for the night.

Foraying into the past, especially into her relationship with Luke always created a mingling of both pain and pleasure. She tried to do it as rarely as possible.

Over the last five years of separation, she'd focused on the pain and had forgotten many of the happy moments they had shared. Danny had made her remember some of the pleasure, and it had been distinctly uncomfortable.

She'd be smart to remember the disillusionment that had accompanied her marriage and divorce. She'd gone into their marriage a starry-eyed romantic with clear-cut ideas of love and marriage. She'd exited the marriage with her dreams shattered and her heart badly bruised. As she'd told Danny, sometimes love wasn't enough, and in their marriage that had been true. The love had somehow gotten buried beneath unfulfilled needs, and banished dreams.

"Here you are," Luke said as he came outside and handed her a fresh cup of coffee.

She murmured her thanks, slightly discomfited as he eased himself down next to her. She felt enveloped by his scent, which rang a chord of bittersweet longing with its comforting familiarity. His leg pressed against hers and she could feel the heat from his body.

"Is he settled in?" she asked, shoving aside the haunting strains of yesteryear. She shifted her position so that there was no physical contact between them.

"I think he was asleep before I finished pouring your coffee." Luke smiled, apparently not noticing her movement to put distance between them. "He's really excited about the Indian reservation visit tomorrow. He's decided for the entire day tomorrow we should call him Little Chief Flying Eagle."

Sherri laughed and shook her head. "He's something else."

Luke's smile faded and he stared reflectively into the dying flames of the fire. "If I had it in my power, I'd do whatever it took to make him capable of flying."

There was a quiet desperation in his voice, a futile need to grant Danny what he wished for most. "I know," Sherri replied softly.

Without thinking, she reached out and touched the back of his hand. Immediately, his hand turned over and warmly clasped hers.

For a long moment, they didn't speak. They sat silently, hands entwined, wordlessly communicating their mutual love for the little boy sleeping inside the motor home. Around them the night spoke in soft whispers, the hushed sound of a light breeze wafting through the trees, the fire crackling as it gasped its final light, the hum of the generator that was providing heat to the R.V.

"I'm glad he has some good memories from our marriage," Luke finally said. "I worried about that for a long time."

Sherri nodded. "That's because we knew when to say goodbye." She was all too conscious of the warmth of his hand surrounding hers. She had always loved his hands, had always felt safe when his had entwined with hers. It was strange, even after all the time that had passed, it still made her feel that way.

It had frightened her just a little, how good Luke's hand felt surrounding hers. She gave it a final squeeze, then withdrew hers from his grasp. "We got out before the real fighting and recriminations and ugly scenes began," Sherri observed softly.

"Yeah, I guess that makes us two of the smart ones."

Sherri nodded, and Luke stood up. "Well, I think I'll hit the hay." He hesitated a moment as she remained where she was. "You coming?"

"In a minute."

He paused another moment. "Good night, Sherri."

"Night, Luke." She watched as he disappeared into the R.V. She tilted her head back and looked at the stars overhead. She could still smell the evocative scent of him. Her hand still tingled with the warmth of his. She suddenly wondered, had they really been so smart? Or had they merely been quitters?

Chapter Four

They arrived at the Indian village the next day just after three o'clock. "We'll need to leave here by five so we can make it to the next campsite by dark," Sherri said as they got out of the motor home. She looked toward the village in disappointment. "Although that shouldn't be a problem. It doesn't look like there's much here." It was obviously a commercial venture, a tourist trap to lure travelers the twelve miles off the highway. "It looks pretty deserted."

"We aren't here in the height of the tourist season," Luke reminded her. "At least there's a couple of teepees," he observed.

There were three teepees, to be exact. The bulk of the "village" was a large, low building that looked as though it sold souvenirs.

Still, Danny didn't seem to mind. He danced in front of the two adults, hurrying them along the dusty terrain. "You think there's some real Indians here? Maybe we'll see a bow and arrow. I can't wait to see a real teepee!" His excited chatter filled the air.

They entered the large building and discovered that half of it was a souvenir shop, the other half was an Indian museum. Luke paid their admittance and they entered through the turnstile and into the museum area.

"Wow, these are awesome," Danny exclaimed as he peered into a glass case that displayed a dozen arrowheads and several wooden bows.

"These are Cherokee artifacts," Luke explained to his son. "The Cherokee were one of the Five Civilized tribes." He grinned sheepishly at Sherri. "I saw a special on television not long ago."

As he explained to Danny about the Five Civilized tribes and the Trail of Tears, Sherri watched him, suddenly remembering his love of learning. His knowledge on a diverse range of topics had always astonished her. He had no formal education beyond high school, yet had never stopped wanting to learn. He read a lot, and had always loved documentaries on television.

He would have made a good teacher, she thought as she observed his patience with Danny, his obvious joy in sharing his knowledge of Native American myth and fact.

Would things have been different between them if Luke had been a teacher instead of a photographer?

Would their marriage have fallen apart if he had gone to work each morning and come home each evening instead of flying off to all parts of the world for indefinite periods of time?

Dangerous thoughts, she chided herself as they moved from exhibit to exhibit. In any case, it didn't matter. Reality was that Luke wasn't a teacher. He was a man who thrived on living on the edge, needed the adventure of exotic places and strange faces.

Reality was she'd always needed more than he could give her, and there was no way to go back and reclaim what they had once had, what had been ruined between them.

Still, as she watched Luke and Danny together, she knew there was a very large piece of her heart that Luke would forever own. As her first love, as the father of her child, he held a place inside her that no other man would ever be able to usurp.

"Hey, Mom, come on. We're going outside to look at the teepees," Danny exclaimed. He grabbed her hand and tugged her toward the door that led to the outside area of interest. "Dad said for us to go on out, that he'd be out in a minute."

Sherri grinned at her son's obvious excitement. "Are you having a good time?"

His blue eyes sparkled happily. "The best." He frowned suddenly, his gaze studying her. "Are you having a good time? I know you aren't too excited about Indians. Maybe we could find a dress shop or something for you to visit when we leave here."

Sherri laughed, her heart touched by her son's worry about her. "I'm crazy about this place and I'm having the very best time." She buttoned his coat, gave him a quick hug, then allowed herself to be pulled out the doorway and into the cold Oklahoma sunshine.

As they walked toward the first teepee, Sherri looked at her watch, surprised to realize it had taken them longer to go through the museum than she'd expected. They'd have just enough time to look at the teepees, then they needed to get on the road again so they could make their next campsite before dark.

As Danny explored the interior of the first Indian structure, Sherri saw Luke approach. For a moment, as he walked across the dusty ground toward her, her heart did a strange loop-de-loop in her chest.

With his long lean legs clad in worn jeans and his tanned features, he looked as if he belonged out here in the Wild West. Even his walk, that hip-rolling swagger reminded her suddenly of a gunslinger from out of history.

Why hasn't he gotten fat, or dissipated from too much alcohol? she thought with a touch of irritation. This whole trip would have been so much easier on her if he'd gotten unattractive since their divorce.

But instead, she found him as appealing as she ever had, with that sexy grin that threatened to steal her very breath away.

"Where's Danny?" he asked as he stopped next to her.

She gestured to the inside of the teepee. "I think he's pretending he's Big Chief Sitting Bull." She looked at her watch, then at Luke. "As soon as he finishes his exploration, we should get back on the road."

"That's what I wanted to talk to you about. There's been a change of plans."

"A change of plans?" She looked at him expectantly, her stomach clenching with nervousness. She hated unexpected change of any kind.

"At five o'clock, they put on a mock ceremonial dance. Danny would love it and since we're already here, we might as well stay to watch it."

"But we said we'd leave here by five," Sherri protested. "Otherwise, it will be too late by the time we get to the next campsite."

Luke shrugged. "So, we eat in the dark, or we stop at a closer camp." His jaw knotted ominously. "Sherri, don't make this into a big hassle. This is really important."

"Dad, come in and look," Danny said as he poked his head out of the teepee.

"Just a minute, son." Luke turned back to Sherri. "We're already here. What difference does an extra hour or hour and a half make?"

"But it will throw us completely off schedule." Panic crawled up into her throat.

"This is a vacation, Sherri. Not some damned schedule we must adhere to." His eyes blazed the cold blue she'd always dreaded.

"But—"

"Lighten up. That's your problem, Sherri. You ruin all the fun with your damned schedules. You've always been so rigid.'' He didn't wait for her answer, but instead turned on his heels and disappeared into the teepee.

Sherri glared after him, a combination of hurt and anger boiling inside her. It was an old fight...one they had practiced too often. Bitter memories swelled in her head. He'd always accused her of being too rigid. "Loosen up, Sherri. Be spontaneous." How many times in their marriage had she heard those words.

He had some nerve telling her she ruined everything with her schedules. He'd ruined their marriage because he could never adhere to a schedule.

She remembered all the dinners ruined, all the plans aborted because Luke had no structure, no discipline in his life. How many hours of their marriage had she spent waiting for a phone call, waiting for him to come home. His impetuousness, his spontaneity had made her crazy, had made her unable to depend on anything in her life. Uncertainty had been the rule of thumb in their marriage, and it had eventually crumbled them.

Oh, yes, he had some nerve. As if demanding his presence for dinner had been her being rigid, had been too much to expect.

She leaned against the wooden railing nearby and watched as Danny and Luke made their way from one teepee to the next.

Although Luke's words burned her stomach like a painful ulcer, she didn't mind staying the extra time for Danny. He'd get a real kick out of seeing a ceremonial dance.

Reluctantly, she pulled herself away from the fence and joined the two males as they left the second tee-pee and headed for the third. "Did Dad tell you?" Danny asked. "There's going to be an Indian dance in just a little while. Dad says we can stay for it. We can, can't we?" His blue eyes reflected his desire.

"Oh course we can," she agreed, rubbing her hand lightly across the peach fuzz on his scalp, which over the last two days had begun to show the dark shadow of new hair growth. "How could I even think of letting Little Chief Flying Eagle miss out on a real Indian dance."

Danny grinned his obvious relief as Sherri exchanged a cool glance with Luke. "This means we'll probably have to eat sandwiches tonight for dinner," she told her son. "It will be too late by the time we get to a campsite to make a fire, or anything."

"That's okay," Danny agreed easily. "We don't have to have a fire and be outside every night, and I don't care what we have for dinner."

Sherri nodded, knowing at least the latter part was true. Danny's appetite hadn't been good for the past several months... a constant reminder of the disease that stole his strength, caused dark shadows beneath his bright eyes, the disease that was the only reason she and Luke were together again... at least for three weeks.

"You aren't too cold, are you, Danny?" Sherri asked, pulling his coat closer around his neck.

"Nah, I'm fine," he exclaimed, dancing out of her reach with excitement.

By the time they had gone through the third teepee, a group of tourists had begun to gather on a small set of bleachers at the edge of a large clearing. "We'd better take a seat," Luke said.

Sherri nodded. She hadn't spoken to him since his comment about her rigidness. She was still angry with him and frustrated because that anger couldn't be vented in front of Danny. As they sat down on the bench, she made sure Danny sat between them, knowing she was being childish, but unable to ignore the stinging hurt Luke had evoked in her.

He'd made her remember their failure, their differences in priorities, the dreams that had been shattered beneath the reality of living together every day.

Worse, he'd made her remember her own faults, her own weaknesses that had played a part in the dissolution of their love.

Initially, immediately after the divorce, it had been easy to blame Luke for the marriage failure. It had been easy to focus on the pain, to point a finger at him. It was only after the first year that Sherri had found the strength to look inward and realize her own culpability.

At the sound of a drum beating rhythmically in the distance, Sherri pulled her thoughts away from the distant past and focused on the building where a group of Indians emerged.

"Wow," Danny breathed in awe, sitting up straighter on the seat to get a better view of the traditionally garbed and painted Native Americans.

Seeing the wonder and excitement on Danny's face made Sherri realize Luke was right. It had been important that they stay and give Danny the opportunity to experience this piece of Americana and history.

She offered Luke a tentative smile, pleased when he gave it back to her. There wasn't enough time to get caught up in the destructive patterns of their past. They didn't have time to fight and hold grudges, to feel bad or entertain regrets and hurl recriminations. There was no time for their personal problems. Danny didn't have time.

With a sigh of relief, Sherri settled back in the seat, her attention torn between the spectacle going on before them and Danny's reaction to it.

It was a fascinating show. The Native Americans performed several traditional dances, amazing everyone with the intricate patterns of movement and difficult dance steps. They explained the traditions and customs that went along with each dance, delighting and educating the audience.

It was nearing the end of the performance when the man in the chief's headdress stepped forward, called Danny's name and asked him to step down from the bleachers.

Danny looked first at Sherri, then at Luke for assurance. When they nodded, he went to where the chief awaited him.

"The Great Spirits in the sky sent me a dream that told me you would be coming," the chief said, looking down at Danny with kind, dark eyes. "They spoke to me of your bravery, of your generosity, of your courage in the face of adversity.''

Danny's thin chest puffed up with pride as his gaze sought his mother's and father's once again. He looked back at the chief, his little body practically vibrating with excitement.

"The Spirits told me of your affinity with flight,'' the chief continued, ''of your desire to soar like a bird in the vast blue of the sky.'' Danny nodded solemnly.

"For this reason, the Great Spirits instructed me to assign you the eagle as your spirit guide.'' The chief handed Danny a rawhide shield with the picture of an eagle hand-painted on it. ''In the name of the Great Spirits, I name you Little Chief Flying Eagle and give you this eagle feather as your talisman against evil.'' He handed Danny a large feather, then smiled. ''And now, Little Chief Flying Eagle will join us in our dance of celebration.''

As the drummers began banging a new rhythm, the chief took Danny by the hand. Sherri's eyes misted with tears as she watched her son trying to match his steps to the intricate movements of the chief's. She swiped at her eyes and turned to Luke. "You arranged this, didn't you?''

Luke shrugged and looked back at his son. "I just explained Danny's situation and they took it from there.'' His eyes were a deep, midnight blue as they turned to gaze at her. "It won't make him well, but...'' His voice broke up and Sherri automatically leaned into him.

As his arm encircled her, she realized how much in the past year she had longed for strong arms to hold her close, to share the burden of her pain.

She now also realized that she hadn't needed just any pair of male arms...she had needed Luke's. Only he knew the depth of her love for Danny, only he knew her rage at Danny's illness. Only he knew the intensity of her despair. He knew because he felt the same way. And there was comfort in the mere act of sharing with him, comfort in being in his arms.

His hand stroked down her back, then up, lingering at the sensitive area just beneath her ear. As his fingers absently stroked, a new, distinctly uncomfortable sensation began to build in the pit of her stomach. She could feel the softness of his fingers, evoking a familiar heat inside her, threatening to engulf her.

"Ah... the camera," she said, desperately scooting away from him and reaching for the case at her feet. Her hands trembled as she removed the camera from the nylon bag. Her neck still burned with the imprint of his caress and she refused to look at him as she steadied herself to take some pictures.

"Here, let me." He gently took the camera from her. "You never could take a decent picture," he murmured.

She watched as he expertly focused and snapped a series of pictures. He caressed the instrument, made love to it as if it were a living, breathing thing. And he got it to perform magic beneath his loving touch.

Just as he's always evoked magic in me with his skillful hands and gentle touch, she thought. A heated blush raced over her features and she tore her gaze away from him.

She exhaled in relief as the performance ended and Danny came racing back toward them. "Did you see me?" he asked, dancing up and down as he clutched his feather and shield to his chest. "Did you see me dancing with the chief? Oh, wow, I'll never forget this in a million years."

Sherri grinned at her son. "I never knew you were so talented. They should have named you Dancing Bear."

"Mom!" Danny exclaimed, but his face shone with obvious pride. "Dancing Bear is a girl name. But Little Chief Flying Eagle is the name of a brave." Again his chest puffed up with pride.

"Well, Little Chief Flying Eagle, we'd better get on the road or we'll never make it to our campsite before the Great Spirits take you to dreamland." Luke threw an arm around Danny's shoulder, then placed his other one around Sherri. Together, the three of them headed to their motor home.

"How come whenever we talk about memories, you never tell any of yours, Mom?" Danny asked. It was nearly ten o'clock and they were seated at the small table, eating ham-and-cheese sandwiches.

"Memories of what?" she asked, noting the dark bruising beneath Danny's eyes, the pinched exhaustion of his features. The day might have been exciting for him, but it had obviously been too much. His shoulders drooped and he'd barely touched his sandwich. He'd also developed a slight runny nose.

"You know, junk like when you were a kid and stuff like that." Danny looked at her curiously. "Dad always tells stories of when he was young, but you never do. How come?"

Sherri leaned back in the chair, a frown furrowing her forehead as she thought back over her childhood. She never talked about it because she didn't often want to think about it. But she could see Danny wanted an answer, deserved an answer. "Sweetheart, my childhood wasn't very happy," she began softly.

"How come? What wasn't happy?" Danny's gaze remained unwavering and Sherri felt Luke's gaze on her, as well. She suddenly realized that in all the years they had been married, she'd never told him anything about her life with her parents.

"My parents were alcoholics, Danny," she finally answered. "They drank a lot...all the time, for as long as I can remember."

"And that made you have bad memories?" he asked curiously.

She hesitated, old images flying through her mind. She finally nodded. "Yes, most of my recollections of growing up are very sad." She reached over and patted Danny's hand. "All my good memories started when I married your dad and had you. Now my good memory bank is full of happy, loving thoughts and times that make me all warm inside."

"I'm glad." Danny smiled sweetly, sleepily. "I want you to always have happy memories of me."

"And now, my little man, I think it's time for bed for you," Luke said gruffly. He picked Danny up in his arms, the little boy curling up without complaint against the contours of Luke's body.

"But I didn't take a bath," Danny protested weakly as Luke placed him on the top bunk.

"That's okay. You can take two tomorrow," Luke said. He tucked Danny beneath the sheet, then walked to where Sherri still sat at the table.

"How about another cup of coffee?" she offered.

"Why don't we take it outside? Danny's already asleep and we can talk for a little while out there without fear of disturbing him."

Sherri hesitated a moment, then agreed. Besides, she wasn't the least bit sleepy. The thoughts of her childhood had made her restless. She poured the coffee and together they went outside.

The motor home was parked near a picnic table and it was there that Luke led her and they sat down across from each other.

Sherri took a sip of her coffee, then leaned her head back and looked up at the skies overhead. The moon was almost full and the stars were bright, appearing to hang so low in the sky, she felt that if she just stretched up high enough, she could capture one in the palm of her hand.

"Why didn't you ever tell me about your parents before?" Luke's low voice split the silence of the night.

Sherri looked at him, noting how the moonlight stroked his features, softened the hard angles and shadowed his eyes. "I don't know...it just never seemed that important."

"Tell me about them now."

She emitted a sharp burst of laughter, surprised by the bitter aftertaste. "What's to tell? They drank and I survived."

"How old were you when they started to drink?"

Memory after memory spilled into Sherri's mind. She closed her eyes for a moment. She jumped in surprise as she felt Luke's hand enfold hers warmly. She opened her eyes, saw that his were sympathetic and suddenly she wanted to tell him, wanted to share the horror of her childhood with him.

"I can't remember a time when they didn't drink," she began. "Some days I'd come home from school and everything would be okay. Mom would be cooking dinner and Dad would be reading the paper and everything would be just fine, normal. Then I'd wake up in the middle of the night to screaming and fighting or drunken laughter and music. I never knew what to expect with them. Just when I thought things were fine, everything went crazy."

She shivered and wrapped her arms around herself, suddenly chilled despite the warmth of her coat. Slices of memories flashed in her mind...coming home from school and finding her mom passed out in the middle of the living-room floor...her dad waking her up in the middle of the night to cook them bacon and eggs because they were hungry.

"The worst part was the uncertainty of it all...never knowing what each day would bring." She released a tremulous sigh. "And when they died in the car accident just after our wedding, I think the saddest part of all was that I couldn't even summon up any grief...they'd lived such a miserable existence." She paused a moment, then added, "I just hope they finally found peace."

"Why didn't you tell me all this when we first started dating?" Luke asked softly.

Again Sherri sighed. "Oh, I don't know...I guess I was ashamed. I got used to hiding it from my friends and teachers. I got quite adept at hiding my parents from the people I cared about." She looked at him, remembering how much she had loved him, how much she had needed him. "I was afraid if you knew, you wouldn't want me, and at that time I thought I'd die if you didn't want me." Her words ended in an aching whisper.

"You should have told me," he admonished.

She shrugged, suddenly exhausted both emotionally and physically. "What difference would it have made?" she asked. When he didn't answer, she stood up. "I'm going to call it a night." She threw her foam coffee cup into the nearby trash container, then turned to go inside. She stopped as he softly called her name. She turned around and looked at him curiously.

He stood up and added his cup to the trash, then approached her. His eyes were soft with regret and an inexplicable emotion she couldn't quite discern. When he stood mere inches from her, he reached out and touched a strand of her hair. He ran its length through his fingertips, then released it and took her chin between his fingers. "It wouldn't have mattered to me, you know." His breath was soft and warm on her face. "I loved you so much it wouldn't have mattered to me if you'd told me your parents were lizards."

A bittersweet pang raced through her at his words, coupled with a shivery thrill of what had once been. For just a moment, a brief second, she felt it all over again...the agony and the ecstasy of loving Luke. She stared up at him, overwhelmed by the burst of emotion that swelled in her heart. Before she could guess his intent, his arms encircled her and pulled her close and his lips descended onto hers. For just a moment, she held herself stiff and unyielding against him. However, as the sweet familiarity of his body beckoned, and his mouth moved against hers with the stir of yesterday's passion, she gave in to the kiss, in to him.

He smelled of the Oklahoma dust, the freshness of the cold and a lingering remnant of his morning cologne, but she found the scent appealing in its masculinity.

Her body molded itself to the strength and hardness of his and she opened her mouth to him, allowing him to deepen the kiss.

As his tongue danced erotically with her own, she felt as if she were seventeen years old again and Luke was the man she loved more than life itself.

The intervening years seemed to disappear, vanish beneath the intensity of the desire he aroused in her. His hands moved slowly down her back as if rememorizing her form. He cupped her buttocks and pulled her closer into him, making her aware of his bold desire.

She was lost . . . lost in a maelstrom of emotions so intense she couldn't think, couldn't breathe. Right and wrong didn't matter . . . regrets and memories didn't matter, the only thing that mattered was being in his arms with his mouth creating magic.

As his lips released hers and kissed along the soft area of her jawline, she released a low moan of pleasure. He abruptly broke the embrace and stepped away from her, his eyes glittering darkly in the moonlight spilling down.

His breathing matched her own, rapid and shallow. "Good night, Sherri," he said, his voice fuller, deeper than usual.

She frowned, her head still reeling. "Luke?" she whispered his name, wanting to be back in his arms, needing him holding her, kissing her.

"Go to bed, Sherri," he demanded. She hesitated, confused by the emotions that still raced through her. "Go on," he urged. "Go before we make a mistake we'll regret in the light of dawn."

His words doused any lingering desire inside her with their dose of reality. She turned and escaped into the motor home with a blush hotly staining her cheeks, her body trembling with need, with want.

She quickly changed into her sleep shirt, checked to see that Danny was sleeping peacefully, then crawled into bed with her unsatisfied longing for Luke as her bedmate.

Of course, he'd been right, she told herself firmly. She turned over on her back and blankly stared up at the bunk over her head. Her body felt heavy and a dull ache throbbed in her lower abdomen . . . the ache of unfulfillment.

She was glad he'd stopped them. Thank goodness he'd had enough sense to realize they were getting carried away, that desire had usurped good sense. Thank goodness he'd been strong enough to stop them from making a regrettable mistake. They'd already made enough of those.

And it would have been a mistake. Making love to Luke again would have been a monumental error on her part. They'd had their chance at love and marriage and had blown it, big time. Making love with him again wouldn't change the past and would only serve to complicate the future.

She'd worked so hard to put him out of her life, worked desperately to become strong enough to live without him. She closed her eyes, trying to forget the burning sweetness of his kiss, the fiery touch of his hands, the hunger he had stirred deep inside her. She turned over on her stomach, wishing the ache inside her would go away.

Still, even knowing that making love to Luke again would have been the biggest mistake of her life, she wished he'd been weak. She wished he'd have let it happen. She also realized she wasn't so strong, after all.

Chapter Five

When Sherri disappeared into the R.V., Luke went back over to the picnic table and sat down on top of the wooden structure, placing his feet on the bench just below.

Damn. Kissing Sherri had been a major mistake. He'd known it the minute his lips had touched the softness of hers, the moment he'd tasted the honeyed sweetness he'd nearly forgotten.

He'd been surprised by her response, and even more surprised by his own immediate reaction. His desire had been instantaneous, fierce and demanding. It had shocked him as his blood rocketed through his veins, taking him too quickly to full arousal.

Damn. He leaned back and looked up at the endless black velvet sky with its diamond chips of stars. For a moment as he'd kissed her, he'd been lost...lost in the pleasurable sensations of time suspended and the heady anticipation of passion sated. He'd momentarily forgotten their past, their situation, why they were together at all.

He'd wanted her. For just a fleeting moment as she'd molded her slender curves against him, as her lips had returned his hot kiss, he'd wanted her more than anyone he'd ever wanted in his life. Until that moment, he'd consciously suppressed the memory of how fantastic sex had always been with Sherri.

It had been her soft moan feathering the hollow of his neck that had pulled him abruptly from her spell. It had been that moan that had cast him back into reality, for it had been that remembered little sound that had nearly undone him. Thank God she had moaned, otherwise he might have taken her right here, in the cold of the night on top of the picnic table.

He released a deep sigh, allowing the last of his desire to expel itself harmlessly into the night breeze. That's where it belonged, dissipating in the atmosphere instead of complicating their lives.

As much as he'd like to indulge himself and make love with Sherri, he knew it would be unfair to her. Sherri was the kind of woman who would expect a commitment, and Luke knew better than anyone that Sherri's level of commitment was stifling, suffocating. He'd tried to live with it once, and it had been a hellish disaster for both of them. Neither of them could afford to make that kind of costly emotional mistake again.

Still, he'd been surprised by her sharing of her painful childhood with him. Surprised and somehow saddened. Perhaps if she'd shared that information with him before, when they'd been together, things might have turned out differently.

He now had a better understanding of her and the things she did. The rigid schedules, the fear of the un-expectedness, the need to control every minute of every day... these were all by-products of living with alcoholic parents. It was the aftermath of growing up in an environment where she had not been in control.

Her statements had brought understanding, and understanding had evoked compassion. Where before he'd always been impatient with her emotional needs, he now understood so much that he hadn't. And along with the understanding and compassion also came a healthy dose of fear.

Dammit, he didn't want to fall beneath Sherri's spell again. He'd always believed you learned from mistakes, you didn't repeat them. In the past five years, Sherri had held a special place in his heart, as his ex-wife and the mother of his son. However, the kiss they had just shared had shaken the benign position she'd occupied in his thoughts. It had removed her from the category of ex-wife and mother and created evocative remembrances of her as a lover and a companion. He realized suddenly how much he'd missed Sherri's friendship. Although in the years they'd been married, he'd often felt suffocated by her neediness, there had been a time when he'd considered her his best friend. They'd shared a lot of laughter...something he hadn't shared much with anyone since.

He braced his elbows on his knees and propped his chin in his hands, his mind once again replaying the feel of her lips beneath his. He'd forgotten her taste, the sweet pliancy of her mouth. She'd always loved to kiss. When they had dated they had often spent hours just kissing...kissing...kissing, until he'd groan and call a halt to the frustrating foreplay. After a date with her, he'd spent many nights standing beneath the stinging needles of an icy shower, trying to cool the fiery flames of want that threatened to consume him.

He stood up and stared at the R.V., easily imagining her lying in the bottom bunk in her fresh-scented sleep shirt, her body warm and supple beneath the material. He emitted a low groan. He needed to forget the kiss. He needed to forget how much he had once enjoyed holding her, caressing her. More than anything, he needed to go inside and take a shower...a very cold shower.

"Danny, don't go too far," Sherri called to her son as he disappeared around a large rock outcropping.

"I won't." His voice wafted to them on the cold, still air.

"I'd better go with him," Luke said, pulling his lanky frame from the lounge chair where he had been sitting. "He shouldn't go off exploring on his own."

Sherri nodded, grateful when Luke passed from her sight. Since the kiss they had shared the night before, things had been decidedly awkward between them.

Neither had acknowledged it, but Sherri was certain he felt the same way she did, that it had been a huge mistake on both their parts.

She went into the motor home and checked the chicken she was baking for supper. Seeing that it was browning nicely, she poured herself a large cup of coffee and went outside.

As she eased herself into the lounge chair Luke had just vacated, her thoughts once again swept back to their kiss.

Since the day they had decided to divorce, Sherri had never looked back. When she'd been young and growing up with her parents, she'd focused on only one thing...survival. When she'd married Luke, she had sought her entire identity through loving him and being his wife. She'd clung to him, needing the kind of security and love she soon knew he couldn't give her. Nobody could.

Immediately after their divorce, she'd realized she didn't know who she was or what she wanted from life. She'd never had the time or the energy to find out.

Since that time, she'd worked hard to make an identity for herself...one that was all her own. She loved her job as a teacher and knew she was good at it. She'd grown comfortable in her aloneness, needing only Danny to fulfill her.

But in that single instant of her lips meeting Luke's, her sense of peace had been irrevocably shattered. She now realized that her feeling of contentment had been an illusion she'd clung to, a false impression she'd wrapped around herself so she wouldn't notice her loneliness. Although Danny effectively filled her life with his laughter and smiles, his incessant chattering and childish wonder of the world, she now knew it wasn't enough.

She missed the sort of soul connection a woman could only feel for the man she loved, those moments when communication could be achieved with a glance, when the touch of a hand could say more than a million words. She missed sharing her dreams with another, being held tightly in the middle of a stormy night, laughing at a crazy bit of nonsense that only they understood. She missed having a lover who could sate her, yet leave her wanting more.

She sipped from her mug, consciously shoving aside these disturbing thoughts. She and Luke were a closed subject. They shared a past and a child, but that was all.

She stirred restlessly and looked around, noting that in the last hour several more motor homes had joined them in the state park campground. She was pleased. She'd been afraid that because of the time of year, they would be the only ones foolish enough to camp. Thank goodness good weather had traveled with them.

They were parked in a new R.V. park less than a mile from the south rim of the Grand Canyon and near a place where helicopter rides of the canyon were offered. They'd arrived at the park before noon, but rather than go on, they had decided to relax for the remainder of the day and head out early in the morning for their exploration of the canyon and all its wonder.

"Yoo-hoo."

Sherri sat up, startled by the feminine voice nearby. She stood as an older woman stepped into view, her silver hair glistening in the brilliant sunlight. She was deeply tanned, wore a fleece-lined bright purple jogging suit and walked with the energetic gait of a woman half her age.

"Hi, I'm Karen Wilson. Looks like we're going to be neighbors for the night." She gestured to the bright yellow R.V. backing into the space next to Sherri's. "The driver is my husband, Barry." She smiled at Sherri, the smile of a woman who had never in her life met a stranger. "Is that coffee you're drinking? It sure looks good."

"Uh...would you like a cup?" Sherri offered.

"I'd love it." Karen plopped down on one of the lounge chairs and swept a strand of her gray hair away from her broad forehead. "God love that man of mine, he got me up at four o'clock to start traveling this morning. He couldn't even wait for me to make a pot of coffee or choke down a doughnut or two."

"I can't help you out on the doughnuts, but I've got a whole pot of coffee in there." She smiled at Karen, instantly liking the woman who seemed to radiate a youthful vitality.

"That sounds heavenly. Barry and I take ours black."

Sherri went inside and quickly poured two cups of coffee, wondering what Luke would think of their friendly "neighbors." She had a feeling he would welcome their presence, especially given the tension that had existed between them for most of the day.

By the time she turned the baking chicken on low and returned outside, Barry had joined Karen. Karen introduced Sherri and he shook her hand warmly, his friendly smile and radiant vitality matching his wife's.

They were just about to sit down once again when Luke and Danny reappeared. "This is my son, Danny, and his father, Luke," Sherri said. Barry and Luke shook hands, then they all sat down.

"Where you folks from?" Barry asked, cradling the cup of coffee between his large hands.

"Connecticut," Luke replied, leaning back in his chair and stretching his long legs out before him. Sherri couldn't help but notice how handsome he looked in his worn, tight jeans and heavy sweatshirt. His face shone with the faint sheen of perspiration from his walk, and for a moment Sherri thought of their sweat-slickened bodies intimately wrapped together in an embrace of passion.

"We're going to fly over the Grand Canyon tomorrow," Danny added, bringing Sherri out of her erotic reverie. She quickly shifted her gaze from Luke and back to their guests.

"Ah, that should be great fun. Barry and I are taking one of the mule rides," Karen said, her gaze lingering on her husband affectionately. "And when we leave here, we're heading for skiing in Colorado. Barry still thinks we're energetic teenagers."

Barry grinned. "You're only as old as you feel." He smiled at Karen, a tender, loving gaze that caused

Sherri's heart to stir with a peculiar throb. "And when I'm with Karen, I feel like a teenager."

Karen laughed, a slight blush appearing beneath her tan. "He's a dotty old man, but I love him."

"So how long you folks here for?" Barry asked.

"A couple of days." Luke placed an arm around Danny, who sat next to him. "As long as it takes for this little buckaroo to get his fill of the place."

"Be sure to see it at sunset. With the pinks and oranges playing on the rock, the view is nothing short of spectacular," Karen suggested. "We've been coming here each winter for the past four years. This time of year, you don't have to fight crowds and the weather stays fairly mild. The canyon is something you can see again and again and never tire of."

"You'll love the helicopter ride," Barry said, smiling at Danny. "The pilots are mostly veterans, good flyers."

"Barry should know, he was a pilot in World War II," Karen explained.

"You were? A real pilot?" Danny leaned forward and looked at the older man in awe. "What kind of planes did you fly?"

"Uh-oh," Karen whispered under her breath to Sherri. "If he starts telling war stories, we might be here all night."

Sherri smiled and settled back in her chair, enjoying the look on Danny's face as Barry began to tell a tale of his days as a flying ace.

Barry was a natural storyteller and as he launched into account after account of his adventures, Sherri found herself as enthralled as Danny and Luke seemed to be.

However, it wasn't long until her attention started to wander from Barry's words to Luke. She watched her ex-husband covertly, enjoying the laughter that wrinkled the corners of his eyes and caused an elusive dimple to dance in one cheek. She'd always loved his smile. She'd once told him that it should be registered as a lethal weapon.

She wondered why he hadn't remarried. He was certainly handsome enough to attract any number of women, but as far as she knew, he didn't date anyone special. Had being married to her somehow soured him on the whole institution? There was a tiny, perverse part of her that hoped so.

It was nearing dusk when she excused herself and went inside to turn off the oven. Although her stomach rumbled in hunger, she was reluctant to call an end to the yarn-spinning. Danny was enjoying the conversation and Sherri didn't want to end his fun.

She turned as the door to the R.V. opened and Luke stepped inside. He smiled at her. "Danny is having a ball. He's fascinated with Barry's stories," he said. "I've never seen him sit so still for so long." He leaned against the counter, far too close to her. She could smell his male scent, feel the heat radiating from his body.

She nodded stiffly, wishing he'd move away. "They're a nice couple," she replied as she busied herself taking the chicken out of the oven.

"I was wondering what you thought of inviting them to eat with us. Is there enough chicken to stretch for two more?"

She looked at him, surprised at his question. The Luke she had been married to wouldn't have bothered to ask her. He would have invited them and let her deal with the problem of coming up with enough food. She frowned, thinking of the chicken, the potato salad she'd made earlier in the day. "Yes . . . I think there would be enough."

He nodded and turned to go back outside. She stopped him just before he opened the door. "Luke?" She placed a hand on his shoulder. "Thanks for asking."

For a long moment, he stared at her enigmatically. "Sure, no problem." He turned and went outside.

Sherri quickly pulled out plates and silverware, then placed the chicken on a platter and took the potato salad out of the refrigerator.

"Knock, knock," Karen called as she opened the door and joined Sherri. In her hands she held a large bowl of fruit salad and a platter of sliced tomatoes. "I figure if we're going to overstay our welcome, the least I can do is contribute to the cause."

"Oh, you didn't have to do that, and you aren't overstaying your welcome," Sherri exclaimed. "However, I accept your contribution." Sherri took the food from her and placed it on the table. "We can fill our plates in here, then eat outside." Sherri smiled. "Danny loves eating outside in front of a fire."

Karen nodded. "Sounds good to me." She glanced out the window where the men were still seated. "I don't know who is having more fun, your son or Barry."

Sherri smiled. "Danny loves hearing stories about flying."

"And Barry loves to tell them." Karen laughed. "God knows, after fifty years of marriage, I've heard them all at least a hundred times."

"Fifty years?" Sherri looked at her in surprise. "You've been together for fifty years?"

Karen nodded. "We celebrated our fiftieth wedding anniversary a month ago."

"That's wonderful," Sherri replied.

"Hmm, I'm pretty proud of it myself. Nowadays, there are disposable diapers and containers, but Barry and I refused to have disposable love...although there were times when it would have been much easier to walk away than to deal with the problems. But we made it through the rough times. Anyway, enough about us . . . I'll call the war heroes in to eat," Karen said.

Dinner was a pleasant affair. Barry and Karen did most of the talking, telling Sherri and Luke of their sprawling ranch home back in Texas, the advertising business Barry had sold when he'd retired five years ago and their travels since that time.

Sherri finally interrupted the conversation as she realized Danny was almost asleep. "Bedtime, my little man," she said.

"Aw, Mom," Danny protested.

"Flying aces have to get their sleep," Sherri replied gently, lifting him off Luke's lap where he had perched after eating.

"Tomorrow night I want to hear all about your helicopter ride," Barry said.

"Okay. Good night, everyone," Danny said as he followed Sherri inside. She helped him change into his pajamas, then tucked him in.

"I like Barry," Danny said sleepily. "He tells good stories."

"I'm glad you enjoyed them," Sherri said, touching the tip of his nose with her finger. "And tomorrow you'll have some flying stories of your own to tell." She kissed him good-night and watched until his eyes closed and his breathing grew regular with sleep.

When she went outside, Luke and Barry had disappeared and Karen sat alone in the semidarkness, her features starkly illuminated by the fire's glow. "What happened to the men?" Sherri asked, joining Karen on one of the lounge chairs.

"Luke talked Barry into a tour of our motor home," Karen answered. She sighed, the contented sigh of a woman well loved. "I'd hate to think what Barry's choice would be if he had to choose between the motor home and me."

"Oh, I have a feeling he'd make the right choice," Sherri said, hoping the envy in her heart wasn't apparent in the tone of her voice. It had been obvious all night that Barry and Karen had the kind of marriage Sherri had always dreamed of having. They'd exchanged warm glances, touched each other often, smiled those special smiles that spoke of love. Fifty years...almost a lifetime together. Oh, yes, how Sherri envied them that.

"I noticed the sign on your R.V.," Karen observed. "The Dream Producers...what exactly does that mean?"

"It's a local charity back home that grants terminally ill children their wishes. They arranged for us to use the van to come here," Sherri explained.

Karen was silent for a moment. "Danny is sick?" she asked softly.

"Danny has leukemia. He's stable right now, but the prognosis isn't good." Sherri was pleased that her voice remained even, not telling of the heartache she carried inside.

Karen released a heavy sigh. "I thought it might be something like that. His hair..."

Sherri nodded. "Chemo is the ultimate barber."

Karen gazed at her, her eyes filled with sympathy. "Have you managed to get past the anger?"

Sherri looked at the older woman in surprise. Most people didn't realize that anger was an emotion that came with the pain and grief.

Sherri laced her hands together in her lap and looked off into the distance. "Yes. At first I was angry. When the doctor first told me, I went through a period of disbelief, then one of incredible anger. I was mad at the doctors and raged at the fates."

Her fingers tightened around one another, a response to the tightness of her chest. "I couldn't understand why this was happening to Danny...to me. What had he done to deserve this? He's just a little boy." Sherri smiled at Karen. "Then suddenly I realized I was wasting all my time and energy being angry, and I still had time left to spend with my little boy. So now we're working to make every day better and brighter than the last...for Danny's sake."

Karen nodded. "That's what you need to do. Make every moment count." Her gaze shifted to the horizon, where the sun was gasping its last breath, painting the sky in deep purples and pinks. "Barry and I lost our son in Vietnam."

She hesitated a moment as if gathering strength and inner courage to continue. "He was eighteen years old...a good boy who had dreams of being a social worker when he got back to the States. God, what a kid." She smiled, the smile fading as tears misted her eyes. "We didn't have a chance to make each moment count with him. We had no idea what the future held. One minute he was alive and well, and the next minute he was gone and all we had was a telegram."

Sherri's heart convulsed in her chest and she reached out for Karen's hand. For a moment, the two simply sat holding hands, silently sharing the bereavement of one mother who had experienced the ultimate loss, and another who would soon experience it.

The fire crackled and hissed, warming the cold night air that surrounded them. Despite the fact that they had only met that afternoon, Sherri felt the bond of motherhood with the older woman.

"It took a long time for me to let go of my anger and bitterness," Karen continued, "and the grief that threatened to destroy everything in my path... including my marriage."

She shifted her gaze from the falling sun back to Sherri. "The best thing you can do is hold tight to that man of yours. Barry and I nearly lost sight of our love for each other beneath the burden of our grief, and that would have been the final tragedy of our life." Karen leaned over and gave Sherri a fierce hug. "You hold onto that handsome husband of yours and you'll be able to survive anything. Trust me, honey. In the end, that love will get you through." Karen stood up and smiled. "And now I'd better get back to that man of mine. We'll see you in the morning."

As Sherri watched her walk away, she realized Karen didn't know that she and Luke were divorced. The older woman had assumed Sherri and Luke were still happily married. And for just a moment, as Sherri leaned back in her chair and relaxed, she allowed herself to indulge in the fantasy that it was so... that she and Luke had never divorced, and when the time came to say goodbye to Danny, she would hold tight to Luke for love and support. They would grieve together and learn to live with their grief through their love.

She narrowed her eyes and stared at the fire, but no matter how hard she tried to focus on the fantasy, reality intruded. She'd already lost Luke, and the thought of losing Danny crashed into her heart and filled her with a frightening void.

The reality was that after this trip, she and Luke would go back to their own separate lives. They were here together only for Danny's sake. Danny had brought them together for this final time. She leaned her head back and squeezed her eyes tightly closed, wondering exactly what was causing tears to burn hot in her eyes...the thought of what might have been, or the thought of what was yet to come.

Chapter Six

"This is the last one," Luke said, handing Sherri a plate he'd carried in from outside. He'd come back from viewing Barry and Karen's motor home just in time to help with the last of the supper dishes.

Sherri took the plate from him and added it to the stack of dirty dishes. "This is quite a surprise," she observed as she placed several glasses in the soapy water and watched as Luke grabbed a dish towel.

"What is?" he asked, taking the clean glass from her and swishing it with the towel.

"I can remember when I didn't think you knew that dishes had to be washed and dried. I never dreamed there would come a time when I'd wash and you'd actually dry."

Luke ducked his head and grinned sheepishly. "It wasn't until our divorce that I realized dishes didn't magically appear clean and in the cabinet following each meal. It didn't take me long to find out there wasn't a fairy who cleaned the dishes overnight. Or ran the vacuum or washed clothes, then hung them neatly in the closet.''

Sherri smiled wryly. "That wasn't a fairy, that was your wife.''

Luke laughed, a low rumble that seemed to echo pleasantly in the pit of her stomach. "That sounds like the punch line to a very bad joke.''

She grinned in response and for a moment they worked in silence, a comfortable silence of unusual camaraderie. Outside, the sounds of night drifted through the walls and mingled with the clink of the dishes and Danny's muffled snoring, all seeming to intensify the cozy aura of the interior of the R.V.

"It was a pleasant evening, wasn't it?'' Luke finally said, breaking the relative stillness.

Sherri nodded. "They're a nice couple." She thought of Barry and Karen and smiled once again. "They certainly give new meaning to the term 'young at heart.'''

"They seem to be pretty crazy about each other," he observed.

Sherri hesitated a moment. "They lost a child. A son in Vietnam." Her words hung in the air.

Luke frowned, wiping a plate slowly, thoughtfully. "That's rough."

"And they just celebrated their golden wedding anniversary," Sherri added, trying to lighten the somber mood.

Luke whistled softly. "Whew. Fifty years...it's hard to imagine, isn't it? That's half a century...five decades." He dried a dish slowly, thoughtfully. "It's hard for me to believe that if we'd stayed married, we'd be celebrating our tenth anniversary next month."

Sherri finished washing the last dish, his comment causing a peculiar wistful pang to niggle at her heart. She was surprised he even remembered that next month would be their anniversary. "It is hard to believe," she agreed softly. Ten years...a kind of milestone in a marriage, but one they had never reached.

Luke took the plate from her, dried it and put it into the cabinet. Then he turned and looked at her, his expression impossible for her to read. "Tenth anniversary...what is that? I know silver is twenty-five and gold is fifty. But what is ten?"

"I think it's tin or aluminum," Sherri said as she pulled the drain beneath the soapy dishwater.

Luke handed her the towel to dry her hands and she noticed that a fanciful smile curved the corners of his lips and a softness warmed his gaze. "What?" she asked, wondering what thoughts caused the pleasant expression to play on his features.

"I was just thinking...if we'd stayed married, what would I have bought you as a gift?" The fanciful expression on his face intensified. "Aluminum foil? Muffin tins?" He shook his head. "Somehow, those don't strike me as being very romantic. I think probably I would have brought you a dozen roses...white ones."

He leaned back against the table, his gaze lingering on her. "And probably you would have spent the day cooking a wonderful gourmet meal and served it by flickering candlelight and you'd have had soft romantic music playing in the background and worn some filmy negligee . . ." The hue of his eyes darkened perceptibly.

His words spun a beautiful fantasy that touched the very core of Sherri's needs and wants. She felt herself leaning toward him, her heart wanting to believe in the image his words evoked. But her head knew differently. Her brain knew it was a false image, one of fanciful visions and desires, painted in the substance of dreams and colored with rose-hued glasses that had nothing to do with reality.

She carefully folded the dish towel and placed it on the counter, then looked at Luke, knowing her eyes held the sadness of truth. "But you know that's probably not what would have happened. In reality, I probably would have cooked a wonderful meal and I might have had romantic music playing on the stereo. Most likely I would be waiting for you to come home from an assignment, and most likely I would have received a phone call from you telling me your plane was delayed or you couldn't get away as expected.

"Eventually, you would have come home late, the dinner would have been ruined and the roses wilted. I would have cried and accused and blown it all out of proportion and we would have gone to bed angry with each other."

She watched as Luke's features hardened and the warm expression in his eyes disappeared behind impenetrable shutters. "You're probably right," he finally said. He raked a hand through his hair, then stood up. "I guess I'll hit the shower and go to bed. If I know Danny, he'll be up before the sun, ready for that helicopter ride."

Sherri nodded and watched as he disappeared down the short hallway and into the bathroom. She sat at the table and stared down at the wood-grain pattern, her thoughts whirling and cascading through her mind.

Had she and Luke been fools? Had they given up too easily? By the time of their divorce, Luke was spending more and more time away from home and when he was home, Sherri had spent most of the time nagging him. Would marriage counseling have helped?

She'd wondered now if she'd ever really fallen out of love with him. Despite their divorce, had there always been a part of her heart intrinsically bound to his?

Regret. For the first time since her divorce, she felt a stir of it in her heart. When Luke had been painting his pretty picture of their tenth-anniversary celebration, she had wanted it to be real. She had wanted it to happen. And not just with any man, but with him... with Luke.

It was crazy, it was insane. She and Luke had been all wrong for each other. Had they stayed together any longer than they had, eventually they would have destroyed each other.

They had become much better people without each other. Divorcing had been the right thing to do. So why did she suddenly feel such regret?

"Luke, here...take the camera," Sherri yelled above the whopping noise of the whirling helicopter blades as she held the leather camera case out to him.

He shook his head, a deep frown wrinkling his forehead.

"Luke...please." Sherri grabbed his arm and shoved the camera into his hands. "Since I'm not going, I want pictures of Danny on his first helicopter ride."

"Sherri...I don't want to take pictures," Luke protested vehemently. He waved to Danny and the pilot who were already seated in the plane. He turned to Sherri and tried to hand the camera back to her.

"This is important," Sherri pressed. "I want pictures of his face, the things he sees." Anger quickly rose to the surface. "Dammit, Luke, why do you suddenly have an aversion to taking photos? God knows you never did in the past."

His features twisted in anguish and his eyes darkened. "Sherri, I've spent most of my life taking pictures of dying kids all over the world...I just can't take pictures of Danny dying...I can't...." his voice broke and he held the camera away from him as if it were an object of abhorrence.

Sherri stared at him, her anger seeping away as she recognized his pain, felt it wing its way through her. She took his hands and pushed the camera against his heart, feeling the solid strength of his muscular chest and his rapid heartbeat. "Luke ... you aren't taking pictures of Danny dying. You're taking pictures of Danny living."

He stared at her. His tormented expression slowly faded and the haunted darkness of his eyes lightened slightly. "Yes ... yes, you're right." He leaned forward and kissed her lightly on the cheek. "Thank you," he said softly. Then, still holding the camera, he ran toward the waiting helicopter.

Sherri watched as the craft lifted off, like a huge silver bird against the early-morning sun. Despite the coolness of the air, her cheek still burned with the imprint of Luke's lips and as the helicopter soared toward the canyon, she reached up and touched the skin that he had kissed. It even felt warm to her touch.

She'd never seen Luke as vulnerable as he had just been. In their years of marriage, he'd always been completely in control, as strong as a mighty oak. Luke strong and mighty was very appealing, but Luke vulnerable was devastating.

She moved over to sit on one of the benches a short distance from the landing pad. Funny, she and Luke had never discussed Danny's illness. Over the past year, since his diagnosis, she had learned to cope, learned to accept whatever the future held, and for the first time, she wondered how Luke was coping.

Luke had been out of the country on assignment when she had first gotten Danny's diagnosis. She hadn't wanted to tell him over the phone, but he hadn't been due back home for another three weeks and she knew she had to tell him. It was the most difficult phone conversation she'd ever had. She'd told him about Danny's illness, her words greeted by a horrible, heavy silence. She'd felt his horror, his grief over the line, but after that moment, although Luke spoke to Danny's doctors, they hadn't really talked about Danny's sickness again.

She somehow sensed that Luke was in a different stage of the grieving process than she was, and she ached for him, knowing the most difficult part ... the final-acceptance part was yet to come. She ached with the knowledge that he would have to go through it alone ... just as she had done.

Leaning her head back, she raised her face to the sun, trying to sort out her confusing feelings toward Luke. She'd begun this trip with a clear picture of her ex-husband, a picture blurred with unpleasant memories and tainted with the bad taste of failure.

Yet, in the days since, the unpleasant memories were slowly fading, being replaced by new memories of her and Luke and Danny together. They were memories she knew would sustain her through whatever the future held.

She couldn't deny that there was a part of her that still desired Luke. When he touched her, even inadvertently or casually, her blood thickened and her heartbeat quickened.

Nostalgia, she told herself firmly. Surely that was all it was. Nostalgia was a strong aphrodisiac, one that created a powerful tug on her heartstrings. Surely it was only the pull of yesterday's memories that kept playing havoc with her emotions where Luke was concerned.

Her mind was merely playing tricks on her... sending her false visions of what might have been ... what could have been had they not given up, quit on their marriage. She'd be a fool to allow herself to start believing the fantasies, in the what ifs.

It would have been easy to fall into the fanciful yarn he'd spun the night before ... easy to get caught up in the spell of what might have happened on their tenth wedding anniversary. But she knew her version was much closer to the truth than his had been. If the past had the power to foretell the future, she had been right in her assessment of what would have happened. She sighed, realizing her introspection was merely intensifying her confusion rather than bringing about clarity. That's the way it had always been with Luke. There was something about him that muddied her thoughts, heightened her senses, made her crazy.

She pushed thoughts of Luke aside and instead focused her thoughts on Danny, and his excitement as he flew over the massive canyon. He was finally getting one of his wishes, he was really flying.

Danny. She had to think about her son. She had to remember that this trip had nothing to do with her and Luke. They were here, together, solely for Danny's sake. And she'd do well to remember that. She leaned forward, eagerly anticipating their return.

''Mom, you should have seen it,'' Danny exclaimed the moment he danced off the helicopter and

ran to Sherri's side. "It was so totally awesome . . . and we were like a big bird flying over it all."
He opened his arms, as if to embrace the entire canyon. "At first my tummy tickled, but then I got used
to the helicopter and it was fantastic." His little face
was flushed with his excitement and his eyes radiated
a reverent awe. "Dad said it took about two billion
years to form the canyon. Two billion years!"

Sherri looked at Luke, who had the same sort of
reverence coloring his eyes. Never had father and son
looked more alike than at that moment. "Are you sure
you don't want to go?" Luke asked her. "It's really a
sight to see." He gestured to the helicopter waiting for
the next passenger to brave a flight.

Sherri laughed. "No thanks. I'm adventurous, but
I draw the line at flying in a helicopter over one of the
biggest ditches in the world."

"Ditch? You're irreverent." Luke laughed. "You
don't know what you missed," he continued with a
grin. "The pilot certainly gave us our money's worth.
He flew us not just over the canyon but down into it."

"Heart failure . . . that's the only thing I missed,"
Sherri exclaimed.

"As we were landing, I saw an observation ledge
that looked like it wasn't too far from here. We could
get a good view from there. Are you game for a little
walk?"

"I am, I am," Danny said, jumping up and down
with enthusiasm.

"Sure, why not?" Sherri agreed.

Together the three of them took off hiking in the direction Luke indicated. As they walked, Danny chattered about what he had seen as they'd flown. He talked of the colors, the reds, the purples, the blues of the canyon walls. He described in detail each and every one of the gorges they'd passed over.

"Dad took pictures of everything. Boy, I can't wait to see them!" he said excitedly.

Sherri smiled, locking the vision of his happiness deep in her heart, knowing there would come a time when it was those visions of joy that saved her very sanity.

She gazed over at Luke, saw the covetous expression on his face as he looked at his son, and knew he, too, was capturing Danny's expression for some distant future.

She thought again of Karen's words from the night before. "Hang onto that handsome husband of yours," she had counseled, adding that it was that love that would see them through anything. Of course, Karen hadn't known that Luke and Sherri weren't married. She hadn't realized that they had divorced and that ultimately they would grieve separately... alone.

Shoving these painful thoughts aside, Sherri directed her attention back to her son, who raced ahead of them as the observation platform came into view. "He'll sleep well tonight," she observed to Luke.

Luke smiled. "He seems to sleep well every night."

Sherri laughed. "I think he takes after his father on that score. It used to make me mad, the way you could instantly fall asleep the minute your head touched the pillow no matter what had gone on in the evening.''

Luke's eyes crinkled at the corners as his grin widened. ''You mean, those dreams I used to have of being beaten were actually prompted by you hitting me over the head with a pillow because I was able to sleep and you weren't?''

His smile reached inside her and coiled around her heart. He had such a beautiful smile. ''I confess,'' she replied, and for a moment she wanted to reach out and take his hand in hers. She wanted to feel the warm clasp of his hand surrounding hers as potently as the warmth of their shared laughter surrounded her heart. She balled her hand into a fist at her side.

''Mom...Dad...hurry up and see this!'' Danny yelled from the platform, effectively breaking the dangerous trend of Sherri's thoughts.

She and Luke picked up their pace, hurrying toward where Danny awaited them. Sherri stepped up on the platform and her breath caught in her chest as she viewed the splendor before her.

The platform hung over the edge of the canyon, giving the illusion of being suspended in midair. All around were the deeply etched walls, the layered colors, the overwhelming magnificence of the canyon.

''It's absolutely breathtaking,'' Sherri finally said, knowing her face mirrored the awed expressions on Luke's and Danny's faces. She pulled up her coat collar against the stiff wind that wafted up from the canyon.

"Isn't it?" Luke agreed. "It kind of makes you feel small and insignificant, doesn't it?"

She nodded, knowing exactly what he was talking about. Staring at the beauty wrought by nature over millions of years, it was easy to realize that man's presence on earth was indeed insignificant...like a mere speck of dust in a cavernous room. Danny's illness, her confusion about Luke, all the problems of living, both large and small, seemed to fade in importance as she gazed over God's architecture in the natural sculpture.

"Hey, look," Danny said, pointing to an outcropping of rocks in the distance. "Don't those look like an old man?"

"Nah, it looks like a naked lady to me," Luke said, laughing as both Sherri and Danny elbowed him in the ribs.

"Over there, I see an elephant," Sherri said, pointing across the canyon.

"Where? I don't see it!" Danny exclaimed, squinting in the direction where Sherri had indicated.

Sherri pointed again, smiling as the men tried to see what she saw so clearly. It was like watching clouds, finding shapes in their cotton-ball whiteness. The canyon with its rugged crevices let their imagination soar.

"Look, Danny." Luke pointed up in the distance where an eagle soared, his massive wings outstretched against the brilliant blue of the sky. Sherri caught her breath at the majestic sight.

Danny watched wordlessly for a moment, then sighed as the eagle winged its way out of sight. "When I die, I won't need a helicopter to fly over all this," he said softly. "I'll use my angel wings."

Sherri's heart convulsed in her chest at her son's words and for a moment she grappled for a reply. As no appropriate words came, she looked at Luke but realized that he, too, didn't know what to say or how to answer.

"It's okay," Danny said, smiling at them both as if he understood their silence. He looked at them with a wisdom far beyond his years, as if his illness had granted him knowledge others still sought. He grabbed first Sherri's hand, then Luke's and squeezed them tightly. "I'm not scared, you know. I mean about dying. I know I'm goin' to heaven and I know I'll be able to fly." He tilted his head, his smile fading. "It will be the baddest for you guys. I'll be all right but you're gonna have to help each other." He took Sherri's hand and linked it with Luke's. For a long moment, he stared at them both, his expression suddenly wistful. "I just wish..." He broke off in frustration. "I wish," he began again. "Ah, never mind." He kicked at the dirt, then stepped away from them and off the platform. "I'm gonna walk back to that water fountain we passed."

Sherri started to follow him, but Luke stopped her. "Let him go. He'll be fine."

She hesitated, then nodded, knowing Luke was right. She leaned against the iron railing, once again gazing out at the natural beauty, but her thoughts were on their son. She knew what he wanted, what it was he'd been unable to say. "You know what it was he was wishing for," she said softly, not looking at Luke.

He moved so that he was standing next to her, his shoulder softly brushing hers. "Yes, I know. He wishes we'd get back together, that the three of us would be a family again." Luke sighed, a heavy sigh that seemed to echo off the distant canyon wall opposite them. "I'd do almost anything in the world for that kid, and I know you would, too." He hesitated a moment and stared off into space. "But there are some things we can't do...not even for Danny's sake. And we'd be fools to get together again just to make him happy."

"I know that," Sherri retorted, finding herself irrationally irritated. The wind suddenly seemed colder, more brutal. "I wasn't suggesting that we actually do it...as if I would want to get back together with you. No thank you. Once was quite enough." She stepped away from him. "I think I'll go get a drink of water, too." Without a backward glance, she stomped away.

Luke watched her go, appreciating the wiggle of her derriere in her tight jeans, the sway of her hair across the top of her shoulders.

She needn't have sounded so damned adamant about their not getting back together, he thought irritably. She'd acted as though the very idea had filled her with revulsion.

And why not? a small voice niggled. He hadn't been the easiest person in the world to live with. He frowned, thinking of the many times he'd been thoughtless, popping in with dinner guests at the last minute, forgetting plans they had made. He'd zipped in and out of the house as if it was a hotel and she a convenience provided for the guests. His work had been all-encompassing, his top priority, and it hadn't been until after their divorce that he'd realized his life was empty. He'd tried to fill the emptiness with his traveling, but even that hadn't been able to fill the void. He missed having somebody waiting at home for him. He missed seeing Danny first thing in the morning and kissing him good-night each evening. But the answer wasn't Sherri.

He leaned against the railing and watched as the eagle reappeared, gliding as if suspended by invisible strings. How long before Danny flew away on angel wings? How long before the disease took him away from them forever?

He consciously shoved this thought out of his mind. Danny would get better. Somehow, some way, Danny would be just fine. They had plenty of time with him. Luke had to keep clinging to that thought, otherwise he would truly lose his mind.

He looked over to where Sherri and Danny stood by the stone water fountain. Even the harsh sunshine couldn't detract from Sherri's prettiness. The brown-and-white-striped heavy sweater she wore made her eyes a rich coffee color and the sun picked up the blond streaks in her hair and made them shine brightly. If anything, she'd only gotten lovelier with the passing five years. The girlish beauty he'd fallen so hard for had matured into something even more splendid.

He'd missed her. The shock of this swept through him, leaving him momentarily breathless. He missed her crankiness when she didn't get enough sleep. He missed her cheerful good morning smile when she'd gotten plenty of sleep. He'd spent the last five years of his life pushing all thoughts of her away. Now he embraced them, let them roll through him with their nostalgic bittersweetness. But it wasn't all nostalgia. It wasn't just thoughts of yesteryear with Sherri that filled him with warmth. It was also being with her now.

He frowned as he remembered that kiss they had shared. She still had the ability to make desire sweep through him like the floodwaters of a burst dam.

It would be easy to give in to Danny's wish, remarry Sherri solely for the boy's happiness. But Luke was a realist, and he knew in the end, it would merely complicate things.

He still cared about Sherri and it would be easy to allow their wish for Danny's happiness and their expectation of the grief to come to force them into making a foolish mistake.

He and Sherri had believed in forever-after once, and that belief had caused them both an enormous amount of anguish.

They hadn't been enough for each other before. There was absolutely no reason for him to think that anything had changed. They would make the same mistakes, feel the same emptiness, and the thought of going through it all over again scared the hell out of him.

Yes, he would do anything in the world to make Danny happy...anything except get involved with Sherri again. That was the one thing he couldn't do...not even for Danny's sake.

Chapter Seven

"Are we ready to head back?" Luke asked as he approached Sherri and Danny where they were sitting near the stone water fountain.

Sherri nodded and stood up, brushing the seat of her jeans with one hand. Gone was the anger that had made her stomp away from him moments before, instead her forehead wore a wrinkle of concern. "Maybe you could piggyback Danny? He's feeling rather tired."

Luke looked at his son, saw the flushed cheeks, the overbrightness of his eyes and frowned worriedly. "You okay, partner?" he asked, leaning down next to Danny.

Danny nodded. "I'm just tired." He smiled crookedly. "And my tummy tickles a little bit. Maybe I just got too excited with everything."

"Well, come on, partner, your dad has a strong back." Luke hefted Danny up on his shoulders.

As they started back, Luke realized the sun had risen high overhead and shone down with gentle warmth, but a wind had picked up, a wind sharp and cold that was near-breathtaking. He hoped the cold wouldn't be too much for Danny. He'd already been fighting a runny nose, and Luke knew his immune system wasn't exactly functioning at a high peak.

Danny's hands rested atop Luke's hair... small hands that held a wealth of trust and love. A shaft of guilt pierced through him and he hugged his son's legs closer against his shoulders.

He'd spent so much of Danny's infancy and childhood traveling the world. He'd missed some of the best times with his son... times that would never come again... times he could never get back. He ached with regret, wishing he could call back those years, those monumental moments of childhood.

Danny had said his first words when Luke had been in Africa. He'd taken his first step when Luke had been in the Middle East. Luke had a wall full of photography awards... and years of missed moments and a deep regret that filled him with emptiness.

He tightened his grip on Danny's legs, silently vowing that from this day forward he would spend every moment possible with his son. He owed it to Danny and he owed it to himself.

He looked over at Sherri, who walked slightly ahead of them. She appeared preoccupied, her forehead wrinkled in thought. The brilliant sun caressed the pale highlights of her hair and the cold wind and exertion of their walk had brought an attractive flush of color to her cheeks. He was again surprised to realize she was still one of the prettiest women he'd ever known.

When they'd first met, it had taken him about ten minutes to fall head over heels for her. It had been a curious experience for him. He'd managed to get to the ripe age of twenty-one without his heart being touched in any way by a woman.

But something about Sherri had tripped him up and he'd fallen hard for her. Not only had she attracted him physically, but she'd had a kind of sweet vulnerability that he'd been drawn to. He'd wanted to cherish her and protect her. Immediately following their marriage, things had been wonderful between them, and Sherri's pregnancy had only heightened their happiness.

So, what had happened? He frowned in thought. How had things gotten so screwed up between them? The first things that had attracted her to him became the things he wanted to run from. Somehow, love had turned to bitterness and bitterness to disillusionment.

Would things have been different had he chosen another career? Worked a nine-to-five job? It was a question that would never be answered.

Strange, he'd never looked back, had felt no regret until the last couple of days. Being with Sherri and Danny had filled a void he hadn't realized was there.

Family. He'd once wanted one, and yet when he'd had one, he hadn't nurtured it, hadn't appreciated it.

He'd made choices that had excluded them, lived a life-style that didn't include them.

Each time he'd gone on assignment, when he returned home he was met with Sherri's accusing silence. She didn't like him traveling. She didn't like the days and weeks of being left alone. She nagged at him to open his own studio and change the direction of his career.

He'd responded by taking longer assignments, finding one excuse after another to stay away from home and the unhappiness in her eyes. He'd retreated from her and her unhappiness had deepened. Finally, he realized they were in a self-destructive pattern that he didn't know how to fix.

The divorce had been his idea, but she hadn't fought him on it. They were softly killing each other, and both knew it. He'd packed his bags and moved out, certain that splitting up was the kindest thing he could do for both of them.

For the first time since their divorce, Luke faced his own culpability in their breakup. He realized that even though Sherri's neediness had been overwhelming, his own choices had merely intensified her insecurities.

Since the time of their divorce, it had been easy to blame Sherri, to tell himself that no matter how hard he tried, he could never fill the bottomless pit of need that Sherri possessed. But the truth was . . . he'd never really tried. When he'd felt inadequate or suffocated, he'd taken another job and flown off to some distant country and the work he knew he excelled at.

And now it's too late, he told himself as their R.V. came into view. Now there was too much history between him and Sherri, too much fear in attempting what had already been proven impossible.

At least he had the comfort of knowing that maybe, if they played it just right, they could regain footing with each other and wind up as good friends. What he didn't understand was why this thought didn't fill him with happiness...it only made him vaguely depressed.

"Home again, home again," he said, shoving his thoughts away as he swung Danny down from his shoulders.

"Jiggety-jig," Danny completed the phrase from the nursery rhyme.

"We'll eat a little lunch, then we can all relax for the rest of the afternoon," Sherri said as they stepped into the warmer air inside the motor home.

They ate a lunch of bologna sandwiches, then Danny decided to take a nap. Sherri and Luke moved outside to sit in the lounge chairs and rest in the shade provided by a small grove of trees.

Luke watched as Sherri opened a book she'd brought with her and began to read. The sun peeked through the leaves of the trees overhead and dappled her features in soft shades of gold. She was wrapped up in a blanket against the cold breeze and her cheeks were rosy-hued by the cool air. He could tell she was completely at ease by the even breathing that caused her breasts to gently rise and fall beneath the cover of the blanket.

He envied her the tranquillity she obviously felt. He was anything but tranquil. His thoughts of the past, of their marriage, gave him no peace. He somehow felt that in order to firmly put her and their past behind—it had to be discussed.

He sat up and leaned toward her, suddenly feeling that it was extremely important to tell her he was sorry...sorry that it hadn't worked out...sorry that they hadn't been capable of filling each other's needs. It seemed crazy, but after all this time, he felt he owed her an apology.

"Sherri?"

"Hmm?" She didn't look up from her book. She turned a page and brushed a strand of hair out of her eyes.

He cleared his throat, searching for the right words...words that were suddenly difficult. Admitting fault was always difficult. He'd never been one to find apologies easy. "Sherri, would you put your book down for a minute? I want to talk to you."

She closed the novel and looked at him curiously. "About what?"

"About our marriage."

Her look of surprise was instantly followed with one of wariness. "What's to talk about? It's long over, part of the past. Nothing is to be gained by rehashing it."

"Perhaps, but this is important. Today while we were walking back, I suddenly realized how much at fault I was in our problems." He frowned, realizing that finding the right words was much more difficult than he'd expected. "This afternoon, I had a sudden moment of self-examination and what I saw wasn't very pleasant.... I guess what I want to say is that I'm sorry."

"Sorry?" She looked at him blankly, as if the word were foreign to her vocabulary.

He sighed and raked a hand through his hair. "I'm sorry that so many of the choices I made when we were married were selfish ones, that I allowed my desire to be a successful and famous photographer to outweigh my need for you and Danny and our life together. I'm sorry that instead of meeting your needs, I ran away from them."

Sherri smiled, a soft, almost wistful smile that attacked Luke's senses, made him want to reach out and touch her, take her in his arms and love her. Instead, he gripped the edges of the chair tightly, effectively checking the impulse. "There was a time when I would have been grateful to hear those words from you, when I would have encouraged you to think of yourself as a selfish bastard who had destroyed our marriage."

She set her book on the ground and sat up, as if needing to face him on an equal level. "Unfortunately, through time and a year's worth of therapy, I've realized that I was every bit as much at fault as you were for the problems we had in our marriage."

"You went for therapy?" he asked in surprise, wondering what else he didn't know about this woman who'd once been his wife. He smiled crookedly. "I knew there were times I drove you crazy, but I didn't realize I'd driven you that crazy."

"Don't flatter yourself," she replied wryly. "I think I was crazy long before I married you." She stared off in the distance, folding her hands together in her lap. He suddenly remembered how she'd always entwined her fingers when she was thinking or stressed. "Luke, I came into the marriage damaged goods, with enough needs and insecurities to form a good-sized mountain. At the time, I didn't realize just how much my parents' alcoholism had affected me. I should have been getting help then, when I was living that nightmare, but I didn't. I married you when I was half a person, and expected you to make me whole. It took a while for me to realize that I had to make myself whole." She looked at him, her gaze clear and calm.

"You've grown up," Luke said, admiration for her newfound strength fluttering inside him.

She smiled. "I'm getting there. I have moments of regression, but for the most part I'm definitely getting there."

"I'm proud of you," Luke observed, noting the way her eyes darkened with pleasure at his words. "But I still can't help but wonder if things would have been different between us if I'd tried to fill those needs of yours instead of flying off into the sunset to escape them."

"Luke, nobody could have filled my needs." She leaned back in the chair, her gaze still warm as it lingered on him. "Perhaps our marriage and divorce were meant to happen. Without them, I might never have learned to depend on myself for my own happiness. One of the nice things that came out of our divorce was that I've realized I really don't *need* anyone anymore. If and when I decide to get into a relationship again, it will be because I *want* it . . . not because I need it." She closed her eyes and raised her face to the late-afternoon sun, as if to signal to him that the discussion was over.

"So am I to gather from your last statement that you aren't presently in a relationship with anyone?" It felt odd, asking her about other men. But it suddenly seemed important that he find out. He needed to know there was no other man in her life.

"I date occasionally, but nobody special." She cracked an eyelid and looked at him. "What about you?"

"The same." It was his turn to smile wryly. "At least nobody can accuse us of rebounding into other marriages. I guess our experience soured us on the institution of wedded bliss."

His words caused her to sit up once again. "I'm not soured on marriage," she protested. "I'm merely more cautious, and certainly more realistic in my expectations." She reached out for his hand. Hers was cool and dry, making him realize that his was clammy and hot.

She squeezed his fingers, then released him and stretched out on the lounge chair. "Actually, I should probably thank you for our divorce. I'm a much healthier person now than I was when we got married.'' She cast him another smile, then once again closed her eyes and raised her face to the sun.

He stared at her for a long moment, noticing vaguely how the afternoon sun had beckoned freckles to appear across the bridge of her nose. Her hair was splayed across the green webbing of the lounger, looking like variegated strands of silk.

She looked like the woman he had married years before . . . and yet he realized that the woman she had grown to be was a virtual stranger to him . . . stronger, with new depths, a person he wanted to get to know all over again.

Sherri didn't realize she'd fallen asleep until she jerked awake with a start. For a moment, she stared around her, disoriented as to time and place. The sun was sinking in the distance, splashing the sky like a painter's canvas. The coming of night and the absence of the sun had brought a winter chill to the air. The chair where Luke had been sitting was vacant and lights were on in the R.V. and radiated into the golden twilight that surrounded her.

She should go inside and see what the guys were up to, but she remained in the chair, thinking back over the conversation she and Luke had just had before she'd fallen asleep.

It was strange how talking about their mistakes, acknowledging their own foibles and accepting responsibility for them had eased the tension that had been ever-present since they'd begun this trip.

Somehow, she felt that in discussing their divorce, they had finally begun the healing process. It was a good feeling. If she couldn't give Danny what he wanted most—a reconciliation between herself and Luke—it would be nice if they could at least give him the pleasure of his parents being friends. And for the first time since their divorce, she thought perhaps a friendship with Luke was possible.

If she could just forget the memories of their lovemaking, refuse to think about the edge of passion that still stirred in her heart for him, then perhaps a real friendship would be possible.

She looked back at the R.V., the lights calling to her like welcoming candles on a dark and stormy night. She pulled herself up and out of the lounge chair, eager to go inside and share the evening with the two men in her life.

"Mom, we're fixing supper," Danny greeted her as she stepped inside.

Sherri stared at Danny and Luke, for a moment speechless as she took in the incredible chaos of the kitchen area. The front of Danny's shirt was splattered with what she hoped was tomato sauce and not blood, and a tiny piece of green pepper clung to the side of his nose. "We're making homemade pizza," Danny announced proudly.

"It looks like you're making a big mess," Sherri observed. She stifled a grin as she looked at Luke, his shirt also decorated with sauce and with a piece of mozzarella cheese hanging from his dark hair.

"I know...I know, pizza is not on your menu for tonight." Luke looked at her expectantly.

Sherri smiled. "True, but that's only because I didn't know you knew how to make pizza." She sat down and stared at the mess.

"We'll clean up afterward," Luke promised, holding up one hand in Boy Scout fashion. "It takes quite a mess to make a world-class pizza."

"You need any help?" Sherri asked.

"Nope, you just sit right there and watch the master chefs at work," Luke instructed. Sherri watched in amazement as Luke and Danny got back to business.

"What do we do now, Dad?" Danny asked, patting the doughy crust he'd been shaping on the pizza pan.

"Now it's time for our special sauce," Luke said, indicating the pan warming on the stove. "This recipe happens to be one handed down in my family from generation to generation."

"Then how come you read it out of the cookbook?" Danny asked with a giggle.

"Shh," Luke hissed as if warning Danny not to give away their secrets. Danny's delighted giggles continued, filling the R.V. with merriment as the two males cooked up their world-class pizza.

It was almost an hour later that Sherri realized nothing made food taste better than the accompaniment of laughter. And there was plenty of it. Luke and Danny worked like a comedy team, causing tears of mirth to course down Sherri's cheeks. Oh, it was good...so good to share laughter with the two of them. Sherri's heart was warmer, fuller than it had been in years.

They lingered at the table long after the whole pizza had been consumed. The feeling of rightness...of family was so strong it seemed to vibrate in the air, an almost tangible force she knew Luke and Danny felt, too. It was magic, the combination of people, place and time that would probably never again be repeated.

Despite Luke's protests, Sherri joined into the cleaning-up process, wanting to be a part of the fun, wishing the night would last forever.

After the kitchen was clean, Danny suggested a game of Monopoly. The pleasant mood and laughter continued as they haggled over real estate. Luke blatantly cheated, moving extra spaces to avoid paying rents or to land on property he wanted to purchase. Sherri and Danny caught him each time and shamed him into obeying the rules.

It was finally Danny who brought the evening to an end. "I don't feel so good," he said as he rubbed his tummy with one hand.

Sherri looked at her watch and gasped. It was nearly midnight. They'd been having so much fun, she'd lost all track of the time. "No wonder you don't feel well," she exclaimed, rising from the table. "It's way past your bedtime. You must be exhausted."

"It's even past my bedtime," Luke replied, picking up the game pieces and putting them away.

Sherri bustled Danny to the bedroom area where she watched as he changed into his pajamas. When he'd crawled into the upper bunk, she tucked him in and eyed him worriedly. "I shouldn't have let you stay up so late."

"It's okay," he said, his hand making small circles on his stomach. "I think maybe I just ate too much of Dad's world-famous pizza."

Sherri placed a hand on his forehead, relieved to find it cool, without fever. "Is it just your tummy?"

He nodded. "I feel like I might throw up. But if I stay real still, I think it will be okay." He hesitated a moment, then continued. "Mom, I'd really feel better if I could sleep all by myself. Can't Dad sleep with you just for tonight . . . please?"

"Danny, that's just not possible." Sherri's nerve endings sizzled at the very thought of sharing her bed with Luke.

She'd managed quite nicely all evening to keep her thoughts of him pleasant and friendly without crossing into dangerous, more intimate thoughts. But the thought of sharing a bed with him definitely filled her mind with dangerous, sizzling thoughts.

"Why?" Danny persisted. "These beds are plenty big enough for you both. Please, Mama, I just want to sleep by myself."

Sherri was torn. Danny had always been the type of child who wanted to be left completely alone when he was ill. Still . . . "Danny . . . I'm sorry but—"

"Don't worry, son," Luke spoke quietly from behind Sherri. "You can have the bed to yourself for tonight. I know what it's like when you don't feel like sharing your space."

Sherri turned and looked at him in astonishment. He carefully kept his gaze averted from hers. He stepped around her and gave Danny a smacking kiss on the forehead. "Sleep well, little man."

"Thanks, big man," Danny said softly.

Luke touched Sherri on the shoulder and indicated that she follow him to the front of the R.V. He immediately held up his hands to still anything she might say. "You can take that panicked look off your face, Sherri," he said dryly. He moved over to the kitchen table. "Don't most of these somehow lower to make extra sleeping space?" He bent beneath the table.

Sherri expelled a breath of relief. She should have known that Luke had something in mind. Surely he was as averse to sharing a bed with her as she was to sharing one with him.

She bent down beneath the table, frowning as she saw the way the table was installed. "It's been customized. It doesn't turn into a bed," she said flatly. "So now what, Mr. Know-it-all?"

Luke grinned. "Then I guess I'll just have to share your bed."

Sherri snapped up with a jerk, bumping her head with a thud against the underside of the table. "Ouch! Don't be ridiculous," she exclaimed. She sat on a chair and rubbed her head.

Luke joined her, sitting near her, the small smile still curving his lips upward. "Sherri, I'm asking to sleep next to you, not with you. We're both relatively reasonable and rational adults. Surely we can share the bed space without any problems, unless..." His grin widened.

"Unless what?" She stopped rubbing her head. Her heart began a rapid thud, banging painfully against her rib cage. "Unless what?" she repeated, her mouth unaccountably dry.

He reached out and lightly traced the veins in the back of her hand with the tips of his fingers, the touch causing a shiver of pleasure to rush through her. "Unless you're afraid."

She snatched her hand away from his evocative touch. "What could I possibly be afraid of?"

He shrugged, his gaze lingering like white heat on her face, then dropping down to caress the rise and fall of her breasts. "Maybe you're afraid that by lying next to me, you'll be overwhelmed with lust and you'll take advantage of me while I'm asleep."

She snorted derisively. "That's the last thing in the world I'm worried about." She flushed and looked away, trying not to remember how he looked in his boxers, trying not to think of the appeal of his naked flesh.

His grin widened. "I thought maybe you were worried that my proximity might overwhelm your senses and cause you to do something foolish. It was always remarkably good between us."

"Only in your dreams would I do something that foolish," she scoffed.

"Ah, in my dreams you are a veritable sex goddess who can't get enough of me." His grin was definitely wicked.

"You are the most obnoxious man I've ever known."

"But the cutest," he replied and despite her irritation, Sherri laughed.

"Tell me the truth, you can't resist me in my red boxers, right?"

"Tell me, do you work hard at being obnoxious, or does it just come naturally to you?" she returned.

He held up his hands in mock surrender. His smile faded and he looked at her seriously. "Sherri, you know I won't be worth diddly tomorrow if I try to sleep sitting up. I know this wasn't part of the original arrangement, but surely we can manage for one night."

Despite her desire to scream and rail, knowing that it was an enormous mistake, Sherri finally nodded her assent. "Just for tonight," she relented. "In future, if Danny doesn't want to share his bunk, you'll have to either fight it out with him or come up with another alternative." She stood up. "Just make sure you stay on your own side of the bed tonight." With this final word, she headed for the shower.

Moments later, standing beneath the spray of warm water, she cursed the fates that had placed her in her present position. She should have refused altogether. She should have told him to sleep on the floor, or sitting up behind the steering wheel. What did she care if he wasn't worth diddly tomorrow?

If she didn't know her son better, she'd wonder if this wasn't some sort of childish scheme to force things between her and Luke.

She stayed beneath the water for an inordinately long time, dreading to leave the bathroom and share the bed with Luke. She stepped out of the stall and quickly dried off, then slipped on her nightshirt. Well, there was nothing to be done about it now. He was right, they were both adults and surely they could share a bed without any problems. After all, they were just going to sleep. It was really no big deal.

Luke was already in bed when she left the bathroom. She turned out the light and slid beneath the covers, careful to hug the edge of the mattress. She didn't want a single toe to touch him.

Despite the distance between their bodies, she could feel his body heat, radiating like the welcome warmth of a furnace on a wintry night. His scent surrounded her, provocatively male and intrinsically Luke.

Her mind suddenly filled with a million memories: wintry nights beneath a pile of covers, Luke's lips warming her body, the night they had made love on their front porch giggling like teenagers as each car had passed on the nearby street, the night she conceived Danny. Memory after memory seared through her mind, teasing her, taunting her with delicious, erotic visions of what they had once shared.

She gasped as his thigh brushed against her own. "Sorry," he murmured, moving away as quickly as she jumped. It was then that Sherri realized sleeping next to him was a big deal...a very big deal. As she lay there, desire hit her square in the middle of the stomach, and along with the desire came a horrifying fact...she was still desperately in love with her ex-husband.

Chapter Eight

She dreamed she was being held in strong arms... arms that made her feel safe and loved. Warmth surrounded her, suffused her, made complete awakeness come slowly, reluctantly. She smiled, content to remain in her pleasant dreamworld forever. So nice...so nice to feel male arms enfolding her close. It had been so long...so very long. She snuggled closer and sighed with contentment. It was the most delicious dream she could ever remember having.

As awakeness came, for a moment she couldn't discern the difference between her dreams and reality. Then she realized she was awake and she was being held in big strong arms...Luke's arms.

She was curled up on her side and Luke was curved spoon-fashion around her back. His body touched her everywhere, creating a coiling warmth in the pit of her stomach. His arm was around her waist, his hand resting on the curve of her breast, as if it had a right to the intimate touch.

His breath was warm as it gently fanned the top of her head and she breathed deeply of the scent that was his alone...the clean, sweet scent of Luke.

Get up, her brain screamed. Get up and get away from him. This isn't good. You shouldn't be in his arms. You're torturing yourself. The tiny voice commanded, cajoled, pleaded, but her body wasn't listening to the logic of her mind. Torture it might be, but it was exquisite. Her body wanted to remain forever in his embrace, wanted the warmth of his body so close to hers. Her body simply refused to move.

She remained completely still, not wanting to break the sweet familiarity and wonder his closeness evoked in her. She remembered other mornings...mornings long ago when she'd awakened in this same position, mornings when she'd turned over and they had made sweet love before they were both fully awake.

She closed her eyes, holding back a deep sigh of sadness, of regret. She wanted to turn over now, watch his eyes flutter open in surprise and pleasure as she stroked the length of his body.

She'd known from the very beginning that this trip was a big mistake. She'd dreaded spending time with Luke, had feared that the close quarters would reawaken the old bitterness, the ancient unhappy memories of yesterday. What she hadn't expected was the reawakening of her passion for him, the rediscovery of her love for him.

Oh, God, how she wanted to awaken every morning with his arms wrapped around her. How she wanted back those Sunday mornings that Danny had remembered, when the three of them snuggled together in the bed and their love for one another had filled the room. She wanted back those minutes... hours... days they had shared... days before things went bad, before their joy had soured.

She squeezed her eyes more tightly closed, knowing such dreams were ridiculous. She couldn't go back and reclaim what might have been. Luke had stated his opinion the other day, when he'd said he couldn't get back with her, not even for Danny's sake.

Her breath suddenly caught in her throat as Luke sighed and stirred against her. The pressure of his hand cupping her breast subtly increased and in horror Sherri felt her nipple tighten and surge as if welcoming his touch. Still, she remained unmoving, allowing herself the luxury of his touch, knowing she was a fool, and not caring.

He shifted, pressing the length of his body more firmly against her back. She could feel the polished heat of his chest, the muscular length of his legs curved into hers, and the potent evidence of desire through the silky material of his boxers.

With one swift jerk, she moved to escape the intimacy... flailing wildly as she fell from the bed and thudded to the floor.

Luke raised himself on one elbow, his blue eyes dancing in amusement. "Good morning," he said and the brightness of his eyes made her wonder just how long he had been awake.

She started to hiss a reply, but stopped as Danny's head popped over the side of the upper bunk. His eyes widened as he spied Sherri sprawled on the floor. He clapped a hand over his mouth to still a bubble of giggles. "Mom, did you fall out of bed?" he asked incredulously.

"I kicked her out," Luke teased. "She's a blanket hog. She was stealing all the covers."

Danny's giggles escaped the confines of his hand. "Sometimes when I sleep with Mom, she steals all the blankets off me and I wake up shivering all over."

"I most certainly do not," Sherri exclaimed, getting up off the floor and glaring at them both. She was relieved that Danny looked fine and whatever ailment he'd suffered the night before had apparently been relieved by a good night's sleep. "And just for that, while I'm dressing, you two are in charge of breakfast." She grabbed her clothes for the day and disappeared into the bathroom.

Once in the privacy of the bathroom, she dressed slowly, trying to still her heartbeat, which continued to race from the effect of awakening in Luke's arms. She took several deep breaths, willing her blood to slow its race through her veins.

They had another ten days left of the trip. Ten days. Surely she could keep her emotions in check for that length of time? Surely she could survive being with him, loving him, and not make a complete fool of herself?

Once they were home, she and Luke would go back to their own lives and eventually she would forget these three weeks, forget that she still loved Luke. All she had to do was make it through the next ten days.

For the first three days, it had been relatively easy for Sherri to keep herself distant from Luke, she reflected upon waking early one morning. They had spent the days exploring, taking hikes in the area and visiting with other campers in the park. The Wilsons had left several days before, Karen giving Sherri a strong goodbye hug as she reminded Sherri to live every moment to the fullest. God knows we've tried, Sherri thought. Each night the three of them had fallen into bed, too exhausted for small talk or dreams.

Luke had confiscated Sherri's camera and spent most of his time taking photographs of Danny... Danny perched on a huge rock, his arms outstretched as if to embrace the entire world, Danny on an observation platform with the splendid canyon at his back, Danny asleep, a smile of pleasant dreams decorating his little face.

They'd been good days...wonderful days, and when her love for Luke had intruded, Sherri had resolutely shoved it aside, refusing to acknowledge it. She wanted nothing to interfere in this opportunity to spend quality time with her son. She didn't want her own weakness and underlying sadness to taint his utter happiness at the three of them being together again like a real family.

Luke had maintained an emotional distance that made it easier for Sherri. He had been pleasant, but there seemed to be a new wall between them . . . one Sherri didn't try to breach. The distance made it easier.

She now crept out of bed, leaving the two men in her life sleeping in the top bunk. She stood for a moment looking at them. Luke was flat on his back, sleeping with his mouth slightly open. She smiled smugly. Danny was in the exact same position as his father, a miniature Luke. For a moment, she allowed her heart to expand with the totality of her love for both of them. Then she quietly turned away and went into the bathroom.

She showered quickly and dressed in the bathroom, hoping she didn't awaken either of them. It was Christmas morning and their last day here. She wanted to fix an extra-special breakfast to begin the day's festivities.

By the time she had placed a cinnamon bread wreath in the oven, she heard Luke up and in the shower. Christmas morning. She stared out the window. It seemed odd to be celebrating the holiday without snow. It was definitely odd to be sharing the holiday with the three of them together. Odd, but so nice. Since their divorce, they had shared Danny on Christmas day. Sherri got him in the morning, and Luke picked him up at noon and kept him until the next morning. It would be nice to spend the day not watching the clock, worrying about shoving all the Christmas holiday into too few hours.

"Merry Christmas."

She turned to see Luke standing behind her, a soft smile curving his lips. "Merry Christmas to you, too." She smiled, suddenly self-conscious and walked back to the oven, checking the raising, browning wreath.

"Something smells good," he said, sitting down at the table.

"Cinnamon bread," she answered, trying not to notice that all she could smell was the scent of his shampoo, the musky sweetness of his cologne. "It should be ready in just a few minutes. Want a cup of coffee?" She didn't wait for his answer, but instead busied herself getting him a cup.

"It seems strange, having Christmas without any presents," Luke said. He smiled appreciatively as she set his coffee before him.

"Danny was insistent, though."

"I know, this trip is all the present he wanted." Luke smiled. "He's a good kid."

"Hey, are you guys talking about me?" Danny stumbled into the kitchen area, rubbing the sleep from his eyes.

"Nah, we've got better things to talk about," Luke teased, drawing the little boy against his legs and rubbing the top of his head affectionately.

"I was just wondering who we could get to put together the Christmas tree that's in a box in the back of the closet," Sherri said, laughing as Danny's eyes lit up.

"You brought a tree?" he asked.

Sherri nodded. "You said no presents, but you didn't say anything about a Christmas tree." She smiled at her son. "Why don't you get dressed and see if you can figure out how to decorate a funky little artificial tree and make it look good."

"Cool!" Danny disappeared into the bedroom.

"I can't believe you thought to bring a tree," Luke said, smiling and shaking his head. "Although it shouldn't surprise me. You prepare for everything."

She looked at him sharply, but realized he wasn't criticizing, only making a statement of fact. "It just didn't seem right not to have a little Christmas with us."

Luke nodded, then smiled. "Remember Danny's first Christmas? We lived in that crappy little apartment on Second Avenue and didn't have enough money for a Christmas tree?"

Sherri sat down across from him, a smile curving her lips. "I remember. You brought home a scraggly evergreen limb and we decorated it with popcorn and tin foil."

"And Danny kept trying to eat the foil."

"And the tree kept falling down and losing needles," Sherri added with a small laugh.

Luke's gaze was soft. "We had some good times, didn't we?"

She nodded, unable to speak, grateful when Danny came flying back into the kitchen with the boxed tree in his arms. As Luke and Sherri watched, Danny put together the plastic tree. Once it was together, he carefully placed the string of miniature lights on the branches, then stepped back and eyed it critically. "It needs something else," he said thoughtfully. He rummaged in one of the kitchen drawers and removed a handful of construction paper, markers, a pair of scissors and a container of paste. "If we each make an ornament, it will make the tree prettier."

Luke frowned down at the paper. "I don't know how to make an ornament," he protested.

"You gotta try, Dad." Danny looked at the two of them, then back at the tree. "This is the first time in a long time that we have a tree that belongs to all three of us. A family tree."

Luke grinned at Sherri and shook his head. "I think we have the makings of a true con artist here."

She laughed and for the next few minutes they all concentrated on making their ornaments. "Dad, you hang yours first," Danny instructed when they were all finished.

Luke had made a Santa Claus in an airplane and Sherri had made a snowman flying a kite. She smiled at Luke as she hung hers, realizing that although they were miles apart in every other area of their lives, they both were closely attuned to Danny and his love of flight. Danny had made a bird, with wings outstretched and he hung it at the top of the tree, then stood back and smiled. "Now it's perfect," he announced. "I think we should sing some Christmas carols."

"Great," Luke said, reaching for Danny's hand. Danny reached for Sherri's, and after only a moment's hesitation, Sherri reached for Luke's other hand, uniting them in a circle around the little tree. They sang for a long time. What Luke lacked in tone, he more than made up for in volume, and most of the singing dissolved in laughter.

By noon, the temperature had climbed out of the thirties and into the forties and they dressed for a final hike. When it had warmed up to almost forty-five degrees and the sun had come out, they left the R.V.

Since today was their last day here before they began the long trip home, they hiked farther than usual, intent on seeing an unusual rock structure that several fellow campers had told them about.

After nearly an hour's hike, they found the structure. They ate a picnic lunch that Sherri had stored in her backpack, then began the long walk back.

What neither Sherri nor Luke had considered was how quickly the weather could change. The sun had disappeared and a frigid wind had taken its place. It now bore down on their bare heads, whistled between them and made the walk seem interminably long.

"You doing okay?" Luke asked, turning around to check on her.

She nodded and pulled her coat around her neck. "I think we overdid it a bit. I definitely smell snow in the air."

Luke nodded and grinned. "What about you, partner? You okay?" he asked Danny, who rode his back like a baby panda bear, his face snuggled into the warmth of Luke's neck.

"I'm okay. I'm just cold and tired. At least we got to see that rattlesnake," he added with exhausted enthusiasm.

Sherri laughed. "Yeah, that really made my day. I'm just glad he didn't decide to stay and eat lunch with us."

Danny giggled. "I think we scared him more than he scared us," he observed.

"As far as I'm concerned, it was an even match on scaring each other," Sherri replied. "I will never turn over another rock in my life." She breathed a sigh of relief as the R.V. park came into sight. "The first thing I'm going to do is make a huge pan of hot cocoa."

"I think I'll take a little nap," Danny said, his face pinched with weariness.

Minutes later, Danny was tucked in for his nap and Sherri and Luke sat at the kitchen table, steaming mugs of the sweet chocolate drink before them. The tiny multicolored lights of the little Christmas tree lent a cheerful sparkle to the kitchen area. "I've never known a nine-year-old who decides on his own he wants to take a nap," Luke observed.

"It used to be a fight, when he was smaller. Since he got sick, he's learned to listen to the rhythms of his body. He knows when he needs rest." Sherri sipped her drink. "I can't believe this is our last day."

"It's gone fast, hasn't it?"

"I just hope this trip has been everything he dreamed it would be."

Luke smiled. "He told me this morning that he'd had the 'bestest' time in his whole life."

Sherri smiled. "I know it's one Christmas I'll always remember." She flushed and looked down at the tabletop. "I'm glad we've had this time together, Luke. Time to put the past behind us . . . let go of the bitterness."

He nodded, his gaze lingering on her face. Clearing his throat, he leaned back in his chair. "It will probably be hard for Danny to adjust to life at home, with no helicopter rides and no Grand Canyon." His unspoken implication was there . . . the fact that Danny would have to adjust again to divorced parents.

"He'll do just fine. School restarts in a couple of days and we'll get back to our normal routines." Sherri leaned back in her chair and looked at Luke. His features were as sweetly familiar to her as her own . . . and yet there seemed to be a new strength etched there, a kind of peace she'd never seen before. Her rediscovered love for him rose inside her, painful in its intensity. She struggled against it. "What about you? Will you be off on another assignment?" She was grateful her voice displayed none of her inner turmoil.

"I don't think so . . ." He stared thoughtfully out the window. "I'm thinking of opening a studio." He smiled reflectively. "Traveling just doesn't hold the same appeal anymore." He looked at her. "You always told me my talent was portraits."

Sherri nodded, her heart clenching in her chest. When they'd been married, she'd dreamed of him giving up his travels and opening his own photography studio. It seemed ironic that he was making that choice now...years too late.

"I'm tired of the traveling. I've been tired of it for some time." Again his gaze went out the window... thoughtfully...soberly. "There was a time when I thought the traveling, the awards, the accolades were all that was important. This last three weeks with Danny has made me see things a little differently." He looked back at her and smiled ruefully. "Maybe I'm finally growing up, too."

Sherri was glad...glad for him. "It will be nice for Danny to be able to see you whenever he wants."

"That's one thing we both did right," he observed. "At least we never used Danny to hurt each other. We never used him as a pawn between us." He reached out and touched the flying-bird paper ornament.

Sherri fought her impulse to reach out and take his hand in hers, fought her need to touch him. "Luke, for every three things we did wrong...we did at least one thing right."

For a moment, their gazes remained locked and Sherri wondered vaguely if her love for him was in her eyes for him to see.

His own eyes gave away nothing of his emotions. They were midnight blue and darkly enigmatic. He scooted away from the table and stood up. "I think I'll go fold up the lawn chairs and get them packed away. We'll want to get an early start in the morning. I just hope we don't hit any snowstorms going home."

Once he was gone, Sherri began packing up the things inside the motor home and getting it ready for travel once again. She'd never thought she'd be sorry to see this trip end, but suddenly she dreaded the ending of what had been such special times together. Like Danny, she had enjoyed the aura of family. She started to take down the little tree, then stopped. She wasn't ready to pack it away yet. It could sit in the center of the table until they got home.

"Mom?" Danny called to her. "Mom, can you come here?"

She hurried to where he rested in the top bunk. "What's up, honey?"

"Mom, I really don't feel good."

"What's the matter?" she asked, eyeing him worriedly. His face was flushed unnaturally red and as she placed a hand over his forehead, she realized he was fevered. His skin was hot and dry.

"I just feel really bad. I'm all dizzy and I feel like I'm gonna throw up." He coughed, a dry, hacking one. "I feel bad, Mom."

"You feel like you're running a temperature. Let me get the thermometer." Sherri's hands trembled slightly as she found the thermometer and inserted it beneath Danny's tongue.

It could just be a touch of the flu, she told herself. Or too much exertion. They'd been going pretty hard the past couple of days.

It could be the onset of a dozen normal childhood ailments, but always in the back of her mind was the fear that it was the insidious disease renewing its grasp on her son.

The thermometer beeped and Sherri read it, her body growing tense as she saw the hundred-and-three degree reading. She placed a hand on the side of his face, noting the dry heat that seemed to radiate from his skin. "You just lie here quietly and I'm going to go talk to your dad," Sherri said.

Danny barely nodded. He closed his eyes, his breath coming rapidly, moving his little chest in an unnatural, rapid rhythm.

Sherri hurried outside. "Luke, Danny is sick."

For a moment, Luke looked at her blankly. "Sick? What's wrong with him?"

"I don't know." Sherri twisted her fingers together. "He says he feels bad and I took his temperature and it's a hundred and three." She choked down the fear that threatened to crawl up her throat. She stared at him hollowly, fighting down her panic. "Luke . . . I think maybe we'd better get him to a hospital."

Chapter Nine

It took only a few minutes for Luke to get them un-hooked from the utilities and pay for their previous usage. While he took care of these details, Sherri studied the material provided by the Dream Producers, looking for the nearest medical facility.

"It looks like there's a park clinic not far from here," Sherri said as Luke pulled the motor home out onto the road. "Go left," she instructed. "And when you get to the first intersection, make a right. If we follow that road, it should take us right to the clinic."

They rode in silence, their concern a living, breathing thing in the air. Sherri worried the map in her lap, trying to fight down her fear. Night was coming and the motor home wouldn't go fast enough to please her. "It's probably just a touch of a flu bug," she finally said, needing to break the heavy silence.

"Yeah, I'm sure you're right. We've been around a lot of people in the past couple of days. He probably just picked up a virus of some kind." There was a quiet desperation in his voice, a need to believe his own words.

They looked at each other...two people with dark hollow eyes mouthing empty words meant to soothe. He reached out for her hand, and she grasped his tightly, their fear not spoken but acknowledged through their fingertips. She wished she could say something, anything to ease the fear that radiated from his hand to hers. But there was nothing she could do but hold tight, her dread eased slightly by the pressure of his hand holding hers.

It seemed like an eternity before they saw the lights of the clinic ahead. Luke didn't release her hand until they pulled up front.

Luke carried Danny in and Sherri followed, clutching Danny's medical charts against her heart. It took the doctor only moments to assess Danny's situation and whisk him away to an examining room.

Sherri and Luke sat anxiously in the tiny waiting room where the doctor had requested they remain. Luke paced in the small confines, his footsteps heavy with the burden of worry. Sherri watched him, knowing her own eyes mirrored the dark torture in his. The waiting room was decorated with red and green crepe paper, and the attempt at holiday spirit only increased Sherri's dread. Had it only been that morning that they had all stood around the little plastic tree and sung carols? Had it only been that morning that

Danny had been smiling and giggling at his father's singing?

Not yet, she prayed inwardly. Please, God, don't take him yet. It's Christmas Day. We aren't ready for this. Give us a little more time with him. Let us love him just a little bit longer. She closed her eyes and repeated the prayer over and over again.

She continued until she felt Luke sit in the chair next to her, felt his hand reaching for hers. She opened her eyes and looked into his . . . saw the fear, the grief that made the blueness appear almost black. She squeezed his hand and smiled with a forced reassurance. "He'll be all right," she said with a confidence she didn't feel.

He smiled gratefully and held tightly to her hand. But it wasn't long before he was up and pacing again, his body taut with tension. "Dammit, what's taking so long?" he finally snapped. "What in the hell can be taking so long?" He slumped back into the chair next to Sherri. Her heart ached, for herself, for Luke . . . for Danny.

She looked up in relief as the doctor walked into the room, his expression inscrutable. Together, Luke and Sherri stood up.

"Please, sit back down." Dr. Michaels waited until they were reseated, then he pulled up a chair facing them. "I've examined Danny carefully and I've read all his medical records." The doctor's smile was filled with sympathy. "I've also run some blood tests and will know more when the results are in."

"Is it the leukemia?" Sherri finally found the courage to speak the word she and Luke had danced around.

"I don't think so, although his weakened condition has complicated things. It looks to me like Danny is suffering from a common cold. In a healthy child, it would be no problem, but Danny is having trouble shaking it off. His lungs are a little congested and his fever is up."

"Will he be all right?" Luke asked, his voice huskier than usual as he leaned forward and looked at the doctor intently.

"We've started an IV and I'd like to keep him under observation for the next twenty-four hours. As long as the blood tests don't show anything startling, I would say Danny should recover without further complications."

A shudder of relief coursed through Sherri, and Luke expelled a deep, trembling sigh. "Can we see him?" he asked.

Dr. Michaels stood up with a nod. "You can spend a few minutes with him. Unfortunately, we're a small facility and don't have the accommodations for the two of you to stay here inside the clinic for the night. However, there are several hookups in the back of the building. You can pull up back there for the night and then we'll see what the next twenty-four hours brings."

Dr. Michaels led them to the room where Danny was already ensconced in a hospital bed, an IV attached to the back of his hand. He looked tiny in the huge bed, his face pale as the sheets. He offered them a weak smile as they entered. "Dr. Michaels told me I'm gonna spend the night here," he said. "What a way to spend Christmas, huh?"

Sherri nodded and moved to the edge of the bed. She picked up his unencumbered hand and brought it to her lips. "Your dad and I are going to park the motor home around back. The doctor says we can't sleep in here with you, but if you need us for anything, you just tell the nurse and she can come outside and get us. Even if you want us to come in and sing some more Christmas carols, you just tell the nurse and we'll be right here."

"Yeah, partner, I'd love to sing some more Christmas songs," Luke said, and Sherri knew the effort he made to force his smile.

Danny smiled faintly. "Dad, I think maybe your singing might make everyone feel worse instead of better." He grinned at Luke's look of mock outrage. "I'll be all right," Danny replied. His eyes fluttered with exhaustion. "You and Dad don't worry about me. You guys got to take care of each other." His eyes fluttered once again. "I just want to take a little nap now, okay?"

"Okay, sweetheart. We'll come back later to see you." Sherri touched his cheek softly.

"Sleep tight, little man." Luke leaned down and kissed his son's cheek. Then together, Luke and Sherri walked to the doorway where the doctor stood.

"I should have those blood-test results in the next couple of hours," the doctor said as they walked down the narrow corridor. "In the meantime, I suggest you both go back to your motor home and relax. I'll send a nurse out when we have the results."

It didn't take long for Luke to move the motor home and hook up to the available utilities. He prowled the small confines of the R.V., his tension swelling in the air. Sherri sat at the kitchen table, wishing there was something she could do to ease his worry.

"I think I'll go for a little walk," he finally said as he yanked on his jacket. "I won't be gone long."

Sherri nodded. She moved to the window and watched his lone figure take off down the road, the gray dusk painting him in somber tones. She sat down at the table, her thoughts still on Luke. He was having a hard time with this. She knew the pain he was battling, the final acceptance he had yet to gain.

He was half her heart, and Danny was the other half, and the thought of being without either one of them seared her with a pain she wondered if she would survive.

She only hoped the doctor was right, and it was just a bad cold at the moment and not a resurgence of the leukemia that plagued Danny.

By the time Luke returned from his walk, Sherri had fixed them a light supper. They ate in silence . . . both waiting for the knock on the door that would signal that the doctor had the blood-test results.

The knock finally came as Sherri was washing the supper dishes. Together, she and Luke followed the nurse into the small clinic and into the doctor's office.

"Good news," Dr. Michaels said in cheerful greeting. He motioned them into the chairs across from his metal desk. "I've got the test results right here and it looks like Danny is holding his own as far as the leukemia is concerned."

"Thank God," Sherri said in a rush of emotion, feeling the tension slowly seep out of her.

"I'd still like to keep him here for the remainder of the night," Dr. Michaels said. "But if he continues to recover tonight, I see no reason that he can't be released first thing in the morning."

"Can we tell him good-night?" Sherri asked.

Dr. Michaels smiled. "I wouldn't have it any other way." He led them down the hallway where Danny awaited their good-night visit.

It was almost ten o'clock when Sherri and Luke finally returned to the R.V. The moment they were back inside, Sherri could feel the tension rippling from Luke. He'd been strangely silent from the moment they'd arrived at the clinic... a silence that had not invited any breach.

But now, body taut as he leaned against the doorway staring out into the darkness of the night, there was something so achingly vulnerable in his stance that Sherri couldn't help but reach out to him.

"Luke?" She placed a hand on his upper arm, felt the muscle jump in response. "Luke, are you all right?"

He sighed, a sigh of vast unspoken sentiment. He turned and stared at the little tree on the table, the lights twinkling merrily, then looked outside the window. "I . . . I've known for a year that Danny was ill, but it didn't really hit me until today . . . until this very moment." His voice was soft . . . a tortured whisper. He shuddered and turned around to face her.

His eyes were blackened pits of torment, and for a moment his mouth worked soundlessly. His features twisted in a grimace of pain so deep, so profound Sherri's heart tore in two. "Oh, God, Sherri. How many more Christmases do we have with him? How many more days do we get?" A convulsive shudder ripped through him once again. "We're going to lose him, aren't we, Sherri? We're going to lose our son." As he said the words, he reached for her and tears spilled down his face.

Sherri's vision shimmered with tears of her own as she wrapped her arms around Luke and held him close to her. Deep, wrenching sobs rent his body, as if they'd been trapped inside him for decades.

In all the years she had known him, she'd never seen him cry. He'd always been her strength, her rock. She knew this time it was her turn to be strong for him. She wrapped her arms around him, digging deep within for the strength she needed.

She led him to the lower bunk and together they sank onto it, still wrapped in each other's arms. Sherri held him tightly, fighting against the tears that burned at her own eyes.

Luke clung to her, his weeping that of a man who'd lost all hope, that of a man who'd suddenly realized he was going to lose his only son and there was nothing he could do about it.

Sherri wished there were words of comfort she could give, but she knew that no words could ease his heartbreak. He needed this cry... the time to talk would come later, when his tears were finally dried and he needed words to fill up the emptiness that was left inside.

His sobs weren't silent, rather they tore from the back of his throat...reflecting the pain that resided in his heart, in his soul. Sherri cradled him like a child, stroking his forehead, patting his back.

He cried for a very long time, holding her as if afraid to let her go. She murmured to him, words she knew he couldn't hear, except perhaps with his heart. She cried with him, for him, for all of them.

Finally, his tears subsided and with an exhausted sigh he fell back on the mattress, his face turned toward the wall. Sherri stretched out beside him, placing her body warmth next to his. She reached out and lightly stroked a strand of his dark hair. She loved the feel of it...like thick silk strands. "Luke?" He didn't answer. "Luke, are you all right?" she asked softly.

He nodded, but kept his face averted from her. "I'm embarrassed, but okay."

"You shouldn't be embarrassed. There's no shame in crying for your son. There should only be shame if you couldn't cry for him."

He swallowed a sob and turned to face her. He sighed, like a forlorn wind filled with winter's chill. "I just wish—" He stopped a moment, then began again,

"I just wish I could get back all the years...all the things I missed with him, all those precious moments of time." He squeezed his eyes tightly closed and when he opened them again, she recognized the emotion that darkened them...guilt. Ah, she knew it well. She had waged many battles with guilt in the past year. She knew well the destructive, defeating pattern of guilt.

"Luke, don't do this to yourself," she said firmly.

"Don't do what?"

"Feel guilty. I went through the same sort of feelings, wondering if I'd fed him differently when he was a baby, would he have been stricken? If I hadn't let him play out in the sunshine, would he have been safe?" Again her hand reached out to stroke his hair. "Danny would have gotten ill whether you traveled or not. And even if you'd have spent every moment of every day with him, the hurt wouldn't be decreased. Besides, Danny would hate us thinking that way."

He sighed. "Logically I know you're right. I just wish...I just wish things could be different."

"Luke, he's not gone yet. We still have him here with us. Who knows, maybe we're the lucky ones." She thought of Karen Wilson, who'd lost her son in a war, who'd had no time to prepare, to be ready. "We know to make each moment count. We know that every second is precious. That's a lot more than other people get."

"But why Danny? Why our son?" The question wrenched itself from him.

Oh, how many times had Sherri asked herself that very same question? "You know there's no answer to that, Luke." She stroked the side of his face. "We can't know why these things happen. And being angry and feeling guilty are self-destructive. In the end, all we can do is come to some sort of acceptance. And make every moment we have count."

He caught her hand in his and brought it to his mouth. Gently, sweetly he kissed each of her fingertips, creating a liquid warmth inside her. "Thank you, Sherri," he breathed softly. He pulled her against him, resting his face in the softness of her hair. "And we will, won't we? We will make every moment count. We will fill each day with enough love to last a lifetime."

"Yes, we'll do that," Sherri promised.

He pulled away from her and she looked into his eyes. They no longer held the deep torment, although there was a sadness she knew he would always carry... as would she.

Before she had time to guess his intent, he reached out and touched her lips with his. She tasted his sorrow. She tasted his desperation. But most of all, she tasted his desire, and as he deepened the kiss, she could do nothing but respond.

Chapter Ten

She opened her mouth to him, yielding with all the love that she'd kept hidden deep inside... with all the love she had tried so hard to deny.

With a groan he deepened the kiss, his tongue delving into her mouth in sweet, remembered intimacy. His arms pulled her closer... closer, until she was molded fully to his length. Without any conscious thought on her part, her body sought to accommodate the familiar contours of his.

Someplace in the very back recesses of her mind, warning signals flashed and caution whispered urgently, but she ignored them all. She wanted to give herself over to the sensations his kiss evoked, the hot liquid fire he stirred as his hand cupped her bra over the material of her T-shirt.

He no longer tasted of grief. Now his lips tasted only of fire... and passion and demand. She moaned with pleasure as he pushed her T-shirt up and moved his mouth down to cover her breast.

She cradled his head, loving the feel of his tantalizing hot breath through the thin wispy silk of her bra. The erotic tongue-flicking caresses caused flames to ignite throughout her body.

Luke. Luke. His name filled her head, her heart. Her enormous love for him expanded in her chest, burned at her eyes, caused a sob of pleasure to catch almost painfully in her throat. She arched against him, needing him, wanting him. And she could feel that he wanted her... needed her, too. His desire, ardent and potent against her only fed her own passion.

When he reached behind her to unfasten her bra, she helped him, arching up to give him easier access to the snaps. Her breasts were freed from the confines of the bra, but were immediately recaptured by the warmth of his palms. His hands molded to her breasts' fullness, his thumbs moving to caress the turgid tips.

He moved away from her only long enough to pull his shirt off. Sherri took the opportunity to take off her shirt, then pulled her bra off and flung it to the floor. He returned to her, reclaiming her lips once again as his broad bare chest pressed erotically against hers.

She ran her hands across the broadness of his back, loving the various textures of his skin beneath her fingertips... the smooth, polished warmth of his shoulders, the hard muscles that radiated from the center of his back. She pressed herself closer, wanting to feel the teasing pressure of his chest against her own, loving the way his chest hair tormented the tips of her breasts. She wanted him to take her, wanted to make love with him again. So much time had passed, so much love filled her soul. She wanted him to take her, possess her forever.

"Ah, Sherri," he breathed as his lips moved across the line of her jaw, down into the hollow of her neck. "Sweet, sweet Sherri," he murmured breathlessly. "You taste so good... you feel so right. I've missed you."

She tangled her hands in the thickness of his hair. She shivered, lost in a haze of desire. Yes, it felt so right...the rightness of familiarity...the rightness of love. And she had missed him, too. She pulled him closer, amazed at how well they still fit.

His tongue flicked at her breasts, teasing first one, then the other rosy tip. Sherri closed her eyes, wanting more...more. A strange contradiction of emotions swept through her. It was like making love with him for the very first time... yet she felt the comfort and easiness of a longtime lover.

She danced her hands down his broad back, reveling in the remembered feel of his muscles. No awkward fumbling, no cautious touches...they were perfectly attuned to each other's wants. It was as if all the years apart fell away, disappeared in a single caress.

She moaned as his lips returned to take hers in a kiss that stole her breath, plundered her soul. She matched him caress for caress, kiss for kiss.

"Sherri . . . Sherri . . ." He repeated her name reverently. "Marry me," he whispered urgently against her neck. "Marry me."

For a moment, she wondered if she'd only imagined the words. She struggled to surface from the fog of passion that made thinking so difficult. "Wha-what?" She pushed against him, looking at him in confusion.

He took her by the shoulders, his eyes fervent, aglow with desire. "Let's get married again. Let's do it, Sherri."

She stared at him, hope crescendoing inside her as his words wrapped around her, seeped through her. "You're crazy," she whispered incredulously, so afraid to hope . . . afraid to dream.

"What's so crazy about it? We're good together. Let's give Danny what he really wants. The two of us together again. Let's do it for him," Luke said.

The hope immediately fluttered and died in her chest and was replaced with a dull, hollow ache. She scooted away from him and off the edge of the bed. "That's not a good idea, Luke. Just because we're good together in bed isn't a reason to rush to the nearest justice of the peace." Her voice shook and tears burned sharply at her eyes. "Sooner or later, we'll have to get out of bed."

She reached down to the floor and picked up her bra. Everything suddenly felt wrong . . . so wrong.

"None of this has been a good idea," she said. Her fingers trembled as she resnapped the bra and grabbed her T-shirt. "I think we let our emotions over Danny get all twisted and out of control. To take this any further would be an even bigger mistake."

Luke sat up and stared at her for a long moment. He closed his eyes and inhaled deeply, then looked at her once again. "Yeah, I guess you're probably right," he finally conceded. He smiled, a small twist of his lips. "But it's still good between us."

"Yes, it is." She didn't have the energy or the strength to argue against what was true. "It will probably always be good between us...but that doesn't make it right."

She turned away, unable to look at him any longer, her heart breaking all over again. She heard him get up off the bed and jumped as he placed his hands on her shoulders. He turned her around, forcing her to look up at him.

"I always heard that asking a woman to marry you was a sure way to get her into bed. Nobody will ever believe that when I asked you, it made the lovemaking stop." He smiled teasingly and she knew he was working to get their relationship back on less dangerous ground.

"You know me, perverse to the end," she said with forced jauntiness.

He looked at her for another long moment, then touched the tip of her nose and released her. "I think I'll go ahead and go to bed."

"Yes, me, too. I want to be up early in the morning to go in and find out if Danny will be released."

Sherri went into the bathroom to change into her nightshirt. She stood before the mirror and stared at her reflection. Her hair was wild around her head and her lips were swollen and bruised-looking.

She looked like a woman who'd just been thoroughly loved. And for the last three weeks, they had all looked like a real family. It was amazing how perceptions and reality could be so different.

She turned away from the mirror, afraid that if she looked any longer she would see a woman crying and she'd shed quite enough tears over Luke.

When she left the bathroom, Luke was settled into the upper bunk. She turned out the light and got into her own bed.

She lay on her back, staring up at the underneath of his bed, her body still entertaining the lingering effects of his potent caresses. She reached up and touched the springs of his bunk, pangs of wistfulness creating a void inside her.

How she had wanted to give in to him, to make love with him. She'd wanted to feel his total possession of her, revel in the wonder of the physical act of love. Her heart, her body, her soul cried out with wanting him.

When he'd spoken those words... *marry me*... her heart had momentarily stopped and she'd had to fight with herself not to say yes.

She wanted to be married to him again, wanted to try it all over again with him. However, she wanted him to want her for his sake... not for Danny's. The words *marry me* could be an elixir for the heart if they were followed by the words *I love you*. But they shouldn't be followed by *for Danny's sake*.

It was happening all over again. She loved him, and the pain of that love was like an arrow in her side. Losing him the first time had been difficult enough. She had a horrible feeling that she would never really be over Luke.

They had forgotten to turn out the Christmas-tree lights, and from the bed she could see them dancing merrily in the darkness. Merry Christmas, Sherri, she told herself. The day that had begun with such laughter, such promise had ended with heartache.

She squeezed her eyes tightly closed and turned over on her stomach. She buried her head into the softness of her pillow and discovered she hadn't lost her knack for weeping silently in the darkness of the night.

"How you doing, partner?" Sherri looked back to where Danny was coloring a picture at the table.

"I'm okay." He looked up at her and smiled. "And you've asked me that a zillion times since day before yesterday."

"That's a mother's job," Sherri teased, "to drive their children crazy by overworrying."

"You do your job good," Danny replied with a giggle, then refocused his attention on his picture.

Sherri turned around in her chair and looked out the window. The landscape was becoming familiar. They would be home in a couple of hours.

Already a bittersweet pang winged through her and she knew she would never be able to look back on this particular vacation without feeling a mixture of incredible joy and overwhelming sadness.

She cherished the time spent as a family, would hold those memories close to her heart. But the sadness would always come when she thought of Luke and this time spent with him. She'd rediscovered her love for him, only to feel the pain of loss once again.

"Anxious to get back home?" he asked her, not taking his eyes off the road they traveled.

"Not exactly anxious, but I am ready to get back to a more normal routine," she said. She smiled. "You know how I love my routines and structure." He smiled in return and she tilted her head, studying his profile. "What about you? Anxious to get back?"

He shrugged. "I suppose I'm ready to get back." He cast her a sideways glance. "Although these past three weeks have been wonderful."

She nodded and refocused her attention out the window. Yes, they had been wonderful and stimulating weeks, and horrible all at the same time.

For the last three days, since Danny had been released from the clinic, Luke and Sherri had gone back to their "safe" relationship. They were friendly, pleasant to each other, but barriers had been erected. For Sherri, the barriers were defensive. She knew she couldn't let him into her heart any more deeply than he was. It was already going to be difficult enough to heal from the scars this trip had wrought.

It seemed as if all too soon and not soon enough they pulled to a halt in the parking lot of Luke's apartment building. "I'd like Danny to come over and spend next weekend with me. Would that be all right?" Luke asked as he shut off the engine.

"Certainly," Sherri agreed.

"What do you say, sport? Want to spend next weekend with me? I should have all the pictures developed by then and we can put together a photo album of the trip."

"Sure," Danny agreed instantly. "That would be cool. Then can I bring the album home so Mom can see the pictures?"

"Of course you can," Luke agreed.

"Here, I made pictures for you and Mom." Danny handed them each a picture he'd drawn. "It's a picture of me... when I'm an angel."

Sherri looked down at the picture of the little boy standing on a fluffy white-crayoned cloud, huge wings stretching out on either side of him.

Her heart squeezed painfully in her chest. She looked at Luke and knew he had a lump in his throat the same size as hers. "It's a beautiful picture," Sherri finally said.

"And see the smile on my face?" Danny asked. "I'll be smiling all the time when I get my angel wings."

Luke nodded. "It's a fine picture, son." He stepped out of the motor home and Danny followed him.

"Then I guess I'll see you next weekend," Danny said and threw his arms around Luke's neck. Luke picked up his son and Danny wrapped his legs around his father's waist. For a moment, they merely held each other, their love a palpable thing between them.

Sherri felt a stinging mist of tears at her eyes as she watched father and son say goodbye. Their love for each other was so strong, and she knew how difficult it was for each of them to part, if only for a few days.

The vacation was truly over. Time to get back to reality, and reality was Luke as a weekend father and Sherri as a weekday mother. Back to separate lives, separate beds and separate dreams.

Luke released Danny and stepped away. He gave Sherri a jaunty salute, then slung his duffel bag over his shoulder and turned and walked away. As Sherri watched, she realized that with him he took her heart.

It could have been different, a small voice whispered inside. You could have agreed to marry him again. However, despite the pain in her heart, she knew the decision she'd made was a good one... the right one.

If they remarried for Danny's sake, and Danny didn't have a forever, then neither could their marriage. She couldn't go through it again. She couldn't marry him, live with him day in and day out, love him and have it all end once more. She was afraid she wouldn't survive it again. It was better this way... better for all of them.

"When are you gonna get cable?" Danny asked as he pointed the remote control and changed the channels on the television.

"I don't know . . . sometime soon," Luke answered as he took the popcorn out of the microwave and dumped it into a bowl. He carried the bowl into the living room and plopped next to his son on the futon. "Surely you can find something you want to watch," he observed.

Danny made another round of the channels, then clicked off the television. "Let's look at the pictures again."

Luke grinned and rubbed his knuckles across the soft hair on Danny's head. Since their return from their trip a month ago, he'd sprouted a healthy head of new hair. "Okay." He got up and grabbed the photo album from the bookshelf, then rejoined his son. "Although I'd think you would have them all memorized by now."

"I just like looking at them," Danny said, opening the album and thumbing through the pictures.

It was all there, a chronicle of their trip together. Picture after picture of special moments saved on celluloid. Luke looked over Danny's shoulder, his gaze lingering on the photos of Sherri.

When Danny reached the end of the photographs, he closed the album and looked around. "When are you gonna get some new furniture? You need some drawers for all those clothes." He wrinkled up his nose and pointed to the pile of clothing in the corner. "This place is a mess."

"Soon," Luke replied. "I've been so busy at the studio, I haven't had time to go furniture shopping. And maybe I should hire a maid."

Danny was silent for a moment. He grabbed a handful of popcorn and popped several kernels in his mouth, crunching thoughtfully. "So when are you and Mom going to get remarried?" he asked suddenly.

Luke looked at him in surprise. "What on earth makes you think that's even a possibility?" he asked incredulously.

Danny shrugged. "You still love her."

"What makes you think I still love her?"

Danny looked at him as if Luke were a complete dunce. "Every time I come over here, you spend the first hour asking me all kinds of questions about her, and that one night when I told you she had a date, you got a real mean look on your face."

Luke sighed, remembering that night quite well. He'd been surprised at the emotions that had pounded through him when he'd heard Sherri had a date. "Danny, even if I did still love your mother, that doesn't automatically mean we're going to get remarried. There are other things to consider."

"Like what other things?" Danny rolled over on his stomach, propped his hands beneath his chin and looked at Luke intently.

Luke felt the warmth of a flush cover his face. "I don't know...things..."

Danny rolled his eyes. "You grown-ups make everything so hard. What kind of things could be more important than loving each other? She still loves you."

Luke's heart missed a beat. "How do you know that?"

Danny crunched a few more pieces of popcorn. "She looks at you like she looks at me, and I know she loves me, so she must love you. Besides, she always asks me questions about you, too." Danny shook his head. "I just don't understand grown-ups. I don't understand what you and Mom are waiting for." He looked at Luke soberly. "You know, it's not like I'm going to be around forever."

Luke stared at his son for a long moment, his heart seeming to stop momentarily in its beating. "Uh . . . I need a drink of water." Luke got up and went into the kitchen, standing thoughtfully against the sink. What was he waiting for? Danny's question reverberated around in his head. Marry Sherri? Why not? He did love her, perhaps had never stopped loving her. And even if he had briefly stopped loving her, it didn't matter. At some point during their trip he had fallen irrevocably back in love with her. Looking at those pictures of her, remembering those moments they had spent together had caused regret to surge within him. He wanted her back in his life . . . not for three weeks, but forever. And Danny was right, he wasn't going to be around forever. Nor did Luke know with certainty how much time anyone on earth had.

He walked back into the living room and faced his son. "Danny, how would you like to go next door and stay with Bill and Linda for a little while?"

"What are you going to do?" Danny asked curiously.

"I think maybe it's time your mother and I had a long talk."

Danny grinned and stood up. "Well, it's about time," he exclaimed.

Minutes later, with Danny staying at his neighbors, Luke drove toward Sherri's house. Was Danny right? Did Sherri still love him?

That night when Danny had stayed in the clinic and Sherri and he had almost made love, he'd thought so. He'd believed that it was love that had sparkled in her eyes. He'd thought it was her heart reaching out to his.

When she'd turned down his proposal, he'd just assumed he'd been wrong, that he'd mistaken what he thought she felt. She'd been trying to comfort him and he'd mistaken it for something more.

Now he was confused... more confused than he'd ever been in his life and he knew the only way to end the confusion was to talk to Sherri.

He looked back on his years without her and saw them for what they were... empty years without meaning, lonely years without her. And somewhere in the back of his mind had always been the thought that eventually he and Sherri would be together again.

But the one thing Danny had made him suddenly realize was how precious time was, and he wasn't willing to waste another minute without Sherri if Danny was right and she did love him.

He increased his speed, anxious to discover if they had a chance to be together again, correct the mistakes and finally find the forever that had been elusive the first time around.

Chapter Eleven

Silence. The house was silent around her. Before the trip, Sherri had always reveled in the silence of the house when Danny had gone to spend the weekend with Luke. She'd spent the time reading, doing needlepoint, watching rental movies she'd particularly wanted to see. However, since the trip, the silence in the house during those weekend visits had been stifling.

Those were the terms she thought in now...before the trip and after the trip. Her life had divided itself into those two time periods.

Before the trip, she had been, if not completely content, then at least at peace with her oneness. Now, even a modicum of peace was difficult to find. She felt only a deep, abiding loneliness.

With a sigh of disgust, she flipped on the television, the room immediately filling with the audience laughter of a sitcom. At least it was noise, she thought.

She could have gone out. Some of her fellow teachers had gotten together to go to the theater and she had been invited, but the invitation had held absolutely no appeal. Besides, the weather was messy. The snow that had been absent in the month of December had appeared in force for the month of January.

However, it wasn't the weather that bothered her tonight, nor was it Danny's absence. She knew what was wrong with her. She was feeling sorry for herself. Today would have been their tenth anniversary—the aluminum or tin one—and she was being a baby and indulging in self-pity and thoughts of what might have been. It was stupid, it was masochistic, but she couldn't seem to help herself.

If she was going to be self-indulgent, she might as well go all the way. She went into the kitchen, opened the freezer door and pulled out the carton of chocolate-chip cookie-dough ice cream. If anything could make her feel better, it was a dish of the sinfully rich ice cream topped with thick hot fudge.

Dish in hand, she returned to the living room and flopped onto the sofa, trying to concentrate on the inane sitcom on the tube. However, the sitcom characters couldn't begin to compete with her thoughts of Luke.

Luke. Since returning home from their trip, she felt the pangs of losing him all over again. She hadn't seen him, had only talked to him on the telephone four times since their return. They were back to their separate lives, with Danny providing their only link.

She started as the doorbell rang. She looked at her wristwatch and frowned. Who on earth would be ringing her bell at ten o'clock on a Saturday night?

Pulling her robe more firmly around her, she opened the door and stared at the man who stood there. "Luke! What are you doing here? Is something wrong with Danny?" Fear clutched at her. Danny had been fine for the past month, but always the fear was there... fear of the disease that hid inside him.

"Danny's fine," he hurriedly assured her. "He's visiting my neighbors."

She looked at him in confusion. "Why is he doing that? What are you doing here?"

"Sherri, we need to talk... but first I want to give you something." He held out a roll of aluminum foil. "It's not the roses I once envisioned, but the flower shop was already closed."

Sherri looked at him blankly, wondering what on earth he was up to...what was going on. She took the roll of aluminum foil, strangely touched that he'd at least remembered their anniversary.

"Can I come in, or do you want me to conduct the heart-to-heart I've got planned right here on the front stoop?" He smiled, that lazy, sexy grin that pierced right through her skin and directly to her heart.

"Come on in," she muttered in confusion. She opened the door and allowed him entry, then led him into the living room. "Are you sure everything is all right with Danny?"

"Danny is fine. Would you take that worried look off your face?" He took off his coat, then flopped onto the sofa, his hand automatically seeking the pulled tuft of material he'd often worried with his fingers when thinking. It was like a blast from the past, merely serving to add to Sherri's confusion.

She sank onto the chair opposite the sofa. "Luke, you want to tell me what's going on...exactly why you're here?" She folded her hands together in her lap and looked at him expectantly.

His fingers caressed the sofa tuft and his forehead wrinkled thoughtfully. "How much do you think we've changed since our divorce?"

"I can't answer that for you...but I know I've changed a lot." Sherri looked down at her hands, then back at him. "Luke, for goodness sake...would you please tell me what this is all about? You show up on my doorstep at ten o'clock at night with a box of aluminum foil and questions I don't understand."

He held up his hand to still her. "Please, Sherri... indulge me for a moment."

She looked at him anxiously, then heaved a sigh of resignation and settled back in the chair. She knew Luke, and when he got that particular look on his face, it meant he was going to do things his own way. Now all she had to figure out was exactly what he was doing.

"I know I've changed," he began slowly, thoughtfully. "My priorities are different. What once was very important to me is no longer important. Did Danny tell you I opened the studio?"

She nodded. "He also told me you already have more work than you know what to do with."

He smiled, a boyish enthusiastic grin that lightened his features and instantly made her heart flip-flop in her chest. "I'd forgotten how much pleasure could be derived in taking pictures of happy, smiling babies and couples in love. I'm finding it more satisfying than I ever thought possible."

"I'm happy for you, Luke. I really am." Sherri tilted her head and gazed at him in bewilderment. She had no idea why he was here, but as crazy as it seemed, she was enjoying his presence. He filled the room with his masculinity. The sofa seemed to shrink beneath him. He'd always complained that it was much too small to stretch out on.

His familiar scent wrapped around her heart, trying to seep through the defenses she had erected. She steeled herself against it, against him, but it did no good. Her love for him was too strong to fight, too deep to overcome.

She wanted a second chance with him. She was a different person than she'd been before. She was stronger, and even though she didn't need Luke anymore, more than anything she wanted him back in her life. She didn't know why he was here, but she refused to guess, to entertain any hope at all. It hurt so much to think of living the rest of her life without him, but she knew it would hurt worse to invite any false hope.

"Now tell me how you've changed," he said.

"Luke, I don't see—"

"You said you'd indulge me in this," he reminded her. "Please, tell me how you've changed since our divorce."

She knotted her hands more tightly in her lap. "I don't know... I'm not quite as rigid as I used to be. I've learned to roll with the punches." She raised her chin and narrowed her eyes slightly. "I've learned to depend on myself, to like myself and most important, I've learned that I don't need anyone but myself." She refolded her hands, her gaze unwavering as it lingered on him. "I don't need you."

His smile froze on his face for a moment, then he slowly nodded his head. "Danny seems to think you still love me."

Sherri felt the blood leave her face and she forced a small burst of laughter. "What does he know? He's just a little kid. He sees what he wants to see, believes what he wants to believe."

"Then it's not true? You don't love me?" He leaned forward, his gaze so intent she felt as if he probed into her very soul.

She flushed and stood up. "This is a silly conversation," she snapped. Dear God, she couldn't tell him. All she had left was her pride. She couldn't tell him that she'd done the stupidest thing and fallen back in love with him. "I already told you I don't need you. What else is there to say?"

He jumped up off the sofa and grabbed her by the shoulders, forcing her to face him. "Just answer the question, Sherri. Do you still love me?"

She stared up at him, wanting to lie, to tell him that she didn't love him at all, that she hated him. She wanted to tell him that her life was wonderful without him, that she didn't lie in bed at night and think about him, dream about him. But she couldn't lie. "Yes, damn you. Yes, I still love you." The words seeped out of her on a sigh of despair. She dropped her head, unable to look at him any longer.

Gently, tenderly, his hand touched her chin, forcing her to look at him once again. A smile curved his lips as he gazed at her for a long moment. "The strangest thing happened on our trip to the Grand Canyon. I began the trip thinking I knew my ex-wife. I knew how she thought, what was important to her. I knew her strengths and weaknesses. But as the days passed, I realized that she wasn't the woman I thought she was. This new woman was stronger, more assured, and the strange thing that happened was that I fell in love with her all over again."

Sherri stared up at him, afraid to hope, afraid to believe what she thought she'd heard. She looked in his eyes, expecting to see a sparkle of humor, the hint of a very bad joke, but she saw nothing except the beautiful blue eyes she loved, would always love.

"I love you, Sherri," he repeated and pulled her against him. "It's crazy and heaven knows it wasn't what I expected, but I do love you." His lips sought to connect with hers.

The kiss, so sweet, so loving...so full of suppressed desire and need finally broke the paralysis that had gripped her.

A sob rose in her throat, choking her as she wrapped her arms around his neck and clung to him. "Oh, Luke, I love you, too. I love you with all my heart and soul."

They kissed again, then Luke led them over to the sofa. He pulled her into his arms, stroking her hair as her cheek lay against his chest. For a long moment, Sherri couldn't speak, so full was her heart. She merely remained in his arms, listening to the sound of his heart beating.

"It's scary, isn't it?" he finally said.

"Terrifying," she agreed. She knew her own heart was beating as quickly, as frantically as his pounded.

He fell silent again, still caressing her hair, stopping occasionally to drop a kiss on her forehead. "Do you think we could make it together this time? You know, if we got married again?"

She pulled away and sat up and looked at him. Her beloved. The man she had loved first...last and always. "I don't know," she admitted candidly. "I think we both have changed...grown up. That's a plus." She reached out and swept a strand of his dark hair away from his forehead. "But we can't do it for Danny's sake. If we decide to try it again, it has to be for our own sake, not for his."

"Sherri, I want to marry you for my sake." He framed her face with his hands, his gaze boring deeply into hers. "Because if I have to spend one more day without you, one more night without you in my arms, I feel I'll go crazy.''

''I feel the same way,'' she whispered, reaching out to touch his strong jawline.

He pulled her back into his arms and for the next hour they talked. They mourned their old dreams... ones that had been shattered beneath youthful self-ishness, neediness and fear. They talked of new dreams... ones that had blossomed from growth, maturity and love.

They spoke of mistakes made and lessons learned and discovered that they had grown into their love. It was a time of healthy healing, and they realized they couldn't completely put the past behind them, rather they had to hang onto pieces of it, learn from it.

''I still make lists,'' Sherri warned him.

''I'll love your lists,'' he replied indulgently. ''And there may be nights I work late at the studio and miss supper.''

''I'll keep it warm for you.''

They spoke of compromise and commitment, and fear slowly faded, being replaced with the certainty of deep and mature love. ''Marry me, Sherri. Marry me as soon as possible,'' Luke said.

''Yes, oh, yes, Luke,'' she replied. ''I want that more than anything in this world.'' She threw herself back into his arms and they kissed in wonder, awed by the second chance they'd been granted.

When the kiss ended, she stood up and held out her hand to him. ''Come on,'' she said. ''There's one more thing we have to do.''

"What's that?" he asked, reaching out to take her hand in his.

She smiled. "We need to go tell our best man that his wish is going to come true." Her tears misted with happiness and she saw that his blue eyes reflected the same wealth of emotion. "We need to tell him that we're finally going to be a family again."

He stood up and gathered her in his arms. They kissed and in his lips Sherri tasted the past, the future... their forever.

Epilogue

"Sherri, it's almost sunset."

Sherri smiled at Luke and nodded. For a moment, she didn't move from the table. Instead, she reached out a finger and lovingly touched the paper bird that nestled in the branches of the little treetop table. Then with a resigned sigh, she put on her coat and picked up an object from the table. She left the motor home and joined him on the observation platform overlooking the Grand Canyon.

As she moved to stand next to him he threw an arm over her shoulder and pulled her tightly against his side. Sherri leaned against him, noting how the lowering sun was just beginning to cast its myriad colors on the walls of the canyon.

"It's hard to believe that it's been two years since we ~~we~~ last here," Luke observed quietly.

Sherri sighed. "Yes, and yet it's just exactly as I remember it. I guess some things never change."

"Oh, it's changed. Subtly, it's changed. The wind and the river have cut the canyon a little deeper, time has stamped its presence on it." He smiled down at her... the smile that still had the ability to make her weak in the knees, cause her heart to stir with overwhelming emotion. "Some things change in that they just get more and more beautiful... like this canyon." He touched her cheek softly. "And our love."

Sherri smiled tremulously at his words, then leaned her head against his shoulder, thinking back over the past two years... years that had passed so quickly.

They had married the Saturday after the night Luke had come to her house. It had been a small ceremony with close friends. Danny had been ecstatic in his role as best man and had guarded the wedding ring like a miser protecting his gold.

Sherri closed her eyes for a moment. Danny...sweet Danny. It had been their son who had taught them the value of time, the preciousness of each and every moment.

For a year and ten months, they had been a family... laughing, loving, living every one of those precious moments together. Last year they'd had the Christmas of their dreams... together. Danny had jumped into their bed, awakening them at dawn. They'd spent the day laughing with one another, loving one another... replacing the memories of the Christmas Danny had spent in the hospital with new ones, better ones.

Danny had been well for a year, eight months and fourteen days, then he had gotten sick again. Even with the visits in and out of the hospital, he'd remained cheerful and accepting, giving his parents the strength to cope, to survive.

Then, a month ago, Danny had gone to sleep and in the middle of the night he'd earned his angel wings. He'd gone peacefully, quietly, with a smile of contentment on his face.

Sherri squeezed her eyes more tightly closed for a moment, allowing her grief to assail her. Luke tightened his arm around her and she knew he was feeling the same emotion.

And now it was Christmas again. Their first without their son. They had come back to the place where they'd rediscovered their love, to say a final goodbye to their child.

She looked up, her gaze seeking Luke's, finding in the blue depths the love she knew would get them through their grief. Karen had been right so long ago. The only way to survive the loss of a child was to hold tight to each other, give and gain strength from the love between them.

She reached up and touched his cheek softly, lovingly, then returned her gaze to the canyon.

They stood for several minutes, watching as the sun sank lower, the pinks and oranges brightening until the sky and the canyon were ablaze.

"It's time," Luke said, his voice a low rumble.

"Yes." Sherri carefully took the brass urn from the large velvet pouch, for a moment holding the container close against her heart.

Danny had been adamant in what he wanted to happen following his death. He'd wanted to be cremated and he'd wanted his ashes thrown across the Grand Canyon at sunset. And he'd made Luke and Sherri promise there would be no tears. Sherri realized now that it would be the most difficult promise to keep.

As she removed the lid, Luke tightened his grip on her. She looked up at him and realized that for the second time in her life she would have to be strong for him. She straightened her shoulders. She could do it. She could be strong for Luke and for Danny.

"It's all right." She smiled at Luke and with his arms still wrapped around her, she turned the urn over and Danny's ashes scattered, winging on the wind and disappearing out over the canyon.

"Fly, Danny," she whispered. "Fly." A sob rose in her throat but she swallowed it.

She suddenly remembered the last day of their trip, when Danny had given them the self-portrait of himself as a Christmas angel.

"I'll be smiling all the time when I have my angel wings." The words swept through her and for a moment she could smell Danny's little-boy scent, feel the essence of his soul as it winged through her, then lifted into the heavens. And for just a moment, the wind sounded like a chorus of angels.

"Look." Luke pointed up against the dramatic sky, where an eagle suddenly appeared, soaring with outstretched wings. It hung, suspended in the air, then with a joyous flap of its majestic wings, it disappeared again beyond the distant canyon wall.

"Little Chief Flying Eagle." Luke's voice was full, deep with emotion.

Sherri wrapped her arms around him and held him tightly. "He's happy now," she whispered softly. "I can feel him smiling down on us...I can feel him here." She took Luke's hand and placed it over her heart.

He shuddered, then slowly nodded. When he raised his head and looked at her, his eyes were clear and shining. "I love you, Sherri," he said.

"And I love you." She wrapped her arms around him as his lips descended on hers. Their kiss was sweet, tender, filled with the abiding love and commitment they'd rediscovered.

They would be all right. What had begun as a trip to the Grand Canyon for Danny's sake had turned into a lifetime commitment for their own sakes.

When their kiss ended, they stayed in each other's arms, leaning against each other. They remained on the observation platform until the colors of the canyon faded with the sinking of the sun. They left a portion of their heart in the canyon, but both knew

Danny had given them a final gift...the gift of their forever together.

And with angel wings and a smile on his face, Danny flew.

*   *   *   *   *

MONTANA™
Mavericks

Stories that capture living and loving
beneath the Big Sky, where legends live
on...and mystery lingers.

This December, explore more MONTANA MAVERICKS with

THE RANCHER TAKES A WIFE
by Jackie Merritt

He'd made up his mind. He'd loved her almost a lifetime
and now he was going to have her, come hell or high
water.

And don't miss a minute of the loving as the passion continues with:

OUTLAW LOVERS
by Pat Warren (January)

WAY OF THE WOLF
by Rebecca Daniels (February)

THE LAW IS NO LADY
by Helen R. Myers (March)
and many more!

Only from ▼ *Silhouette*® where passion lives.

**HE'S MORE THAN A MAN,
HE'S ONE OF OUR**

IDEAL DAD
Elizabeth August

Eight-year-old Jeremy Galvin knew Murdock Parnell would make the perfect dad. Now it was up to Murdock to persuade Jeremy's mom, Irene, that he was the ideal husband for her.

Ideal Dad, available in January, is the third book in Elizabeth August's bestselling series, WHERE THE HEART IS.

Look for *Ideal Dad* by Elizabeth August—available in January.

Fall in love with our Fabulous Fathers!

Silhouette
R O M A N C E™

FF195

Silhouette ROMANCE™

BELIEVING IN MIRACLES
by
Linda Varner

Carpenter Andy Fulbright and Honorine "Honey" Truman had all the criteria for a perfect marriage—they liked and respected each other, they desired and needed each other...and *neither* one loved the other! But with the help of some mistletoe and two young elves, these two might learn to believe in the miracle of Christmas....

BELIEVING IN MIRACLES is the second book in Linda Varner's MR. RIGHT, INC., a heartwarming series about three hardworking bachelors in the building trade who find love at first sight—construction site, that is!

Don't miss BELIEVING IN MIRACLES, available in December. And look for Book 3, WIFE MOST UNLIKELY, in March 1995. Read along as old friends make the difficult transition to lovers....

Only from Silhouette®

where passion lives.

Those Harris boys are back in book three of...

WEDDING WAGER

by Sandra Steffen

Three sexy, single brothers bet they'll never say "I do."
But the Harris boys are about to discover their vows of bachelor-
hood don't stand a chance against the forces of love!

You met Mitch in BACHELOR DADDY #1028 (8/94) and Kyle in
BACHELOR AT THE WEDDING #1045 (11/94). Now it's time for
brother Taylor to take the marriage plunge in—

EXPECTANT BACHELOR #1056 (1/95): When Gina Jenson sets
out to seduce the handsome Taylor, he's in for the surprise of his
life. Because Gina wants him to father her child!